Richard Le Gallienne

The Quest of the Golden Girl

Richard Le Gallienne

The Quest of the Golden Girl

ISBN/EAN: 9783337007898

Printed in Europe, USA, Canada, Australia, Japan

Cover: Foto ©Andreas Hilbeck / pixelio.de

More available books at **www.hansebooks.com**

THE .QUEST OF THE GOLDEN GIRL .

A ROMANCE BY

RICHARD LE GALLIENNE

JOHN LANE: THE BODLEY HEAD
LONDON AND NEW YORK
1900

FOURTEENTH EDITION.

𝔘𝔫𝔦𝔟𝔢𝔯𝔰𝔦𝔱𝔶 𝔓𝔯𝔢𝔰𝔰:
JOHN WILSON AND SON, CAMBRIDGE, U. S. A.

CONTENTS

BOOK I

CONTENTS

BOOK II

CONTENTS

BOOK III

CONTENTS

BOOK IV

THE POSTSCRIPT TO A PILGRIMAGE

BOOK I

CHAPTER I

AN OLD HOUSE AND ITS BACHELOR

WHEN the knell of my thirtieth birthday sounded, I suddenly realised, with a desolate feeling at the heart, that I was alone in the world. It was true I had many and good friends, and I was blessed with interests and occupations which I had often declared sufficient to satisfy any not too exacting human being. Moreover, a small but sufficient competency was mine, allowing me reasonable comforts, and the luxuries of a small but choice library, and a small but choice garden. These heavenly blessings had seemed more than enough for nearly five years, during which the good sister and I had kept house together, leading a life of tranquil happy days. Friends and books and flowers! It was, we said, a good world, and I, simpleton, — pretty and dainty as Margaret was, — deemed it would go on forever. But, alas! one day came a Faust into our garden, — a good Faust, with no friend Mephistopheles, — and took Margaret from me. It is but a month since they were married, and the rice still lingers in the crevices of the pathway down to the quaint old iron-work gate. Yes! they have gone off to spend their honeymoon, and Margaret has written to me twice to say how happy they are together in the Hesperides. Dear happiness! Selfish, indeed, were he who would envy you one petal of that wonderful rose — Rosa Mundi — God has given you to gather.

But, all the same, the reader will admit that it must be lonely for me, and not another sister left to take pity on me, all somewhere happily settled down in the Fortunate Isles.

Poor lonely old house! do you, too, miss the light step of your mistress? No longer shall her little silken figure flit up and down

your quiet staircases, no more deck out your
silent rooms with flowers, humming the
while some happy little song.

The little piano is dumb night after night,
its candles unlighted, and there is no one to
play Chopin to us now as the day dies, and
the shadows stoop out of their corners to
listen in vain.   Old house, old house!   We
are alone, quite alone, — there is no mistake
about that, — and the soul has gone out of
both of us.   And as for the garden, there is
no company there; that is loneliest of all.
The very sunlight looks desolation, falling
through the thick-blossoming apple-trees as
through the chinks and crevices of deserted
Egyptian cities.

While as for the books — well, never talk
to me again about the companionship of
books!   For just when one needs them most
of all they seem suddenly to have grown
dull and unsympathetic, not a word of comfort, not a charm anywhere in them to make
us forget the slow-moving hours; whereas,
when Margaret was here — but it is of no
use to say any more!   Everything was quite
different when Margaret was here: that is

enough. Margaret has gone away to the Fortunate Isles. Of course she 'll come to see us now and again; but it won't be the same thing. Yes! old echoing silent House of Joy that is Gone, we are quite alone. Now, what is to be done?

CHAPTER II

IN WHICH I DECIDE TO GO ON PILGRIMAGE

THOUGH I have this bad habit of soliloquising, and indeed am absurd enough to attempt conversation with a house, yet the reader must realise from the beginning that I am still quite a young man. I talked a little just now as though I were an octogenarian. Actually, as I said, I am but just gone thirty, and I may reasonably regard life, as the saying is, all before me. I was a little down-hearted when I wrote yesterday. Besides, I wrote at the end of the afternoon, a melancholy time. The morning is the time to write. We are all — that is, those of us who sleep well — optimists in the morning. And the world is sad enough without our writing books to make it sadder. The rest of this book, I promise you, shall be written of a morning. This book! oh, yes, I for-

got!—I am going to write a book. A book
about what? Well, that must be as God
wills. But listen! As I lay in bed this
morning between sleeping and waking, an
idea came riding on a sunbeam into my
room, —a mad, whimsical idea, but one that
suits my mood; and put briefly, it is this:
how is it that I, a not unpresentable young
man, a man not without accomplishments
or experience, should have gone all these
years without finding that

> " Not impossible she
> Who shall command my heart and me," —

without meeting at some turning of the
way the mystical Golden Girl, — without,
in short, finding a wife?

"Then," suggested the idea, with a blush
for its own absurdity, "why not go on pilgrimage and seek her? I don't believe
you'll find her. She isn't usually found
after thirty. But you'll no doubt have good
fun by the way, and fall in with many pleasant adventures."

"A brave idea, indeed!" I cried. "By
Heaven, I will take stick and knapsack and

walk right away from my own front door, right away where the road leads, and see what happens." And now, if the reader please, we will make a start.

CHAPTER III

AN INDICTMENT OF SPRING

"MARRY! an odd adventure!" I said to myself, as I stepped along in the spring morning air; for, being a pilgrim, I was involuntarily in a mediæval frame of mind, and "Marry! an odd adventure!" came to my lips as though I had been one of that famous company that once started from the Tabard on a day in spring.

It had been the spring, it will be remembered, that had prompted them to go on pilgrimage; and me, too, the spring was filling with strange, undefinable longings, and though I flattered myself that I had set out in pursuance of a definitely taken resolve, I had really no more freedom in the matter than the children who followed at the heels of the mad piper.

A mad piper, indeed, this spring, with his wonderful lying music, — ever lying, yet ever convincing, for when was Spring known to keep his word? Yet year after year we give eager belief to his promises. He may have consistently broken them for fifty years, yet. this year he will keep them. This year the dream will come true, the ship come home. This year the very dead we have loved shall come back to us again: for Spring can even lie like that. There is nothing he will not promise the poor hungry human heart, with his innocent-looking daisies and those practised liars the birds. Why, one branch of hawthorn against the sky promises more than all the summers of time can pay, and a pond ablaze with yellow lilies awakens such answering splendours and enchantments in mortal bosoms, — blazons, it would seem, so august a message from the hidden heart of the world, — that ever afterwards, for one who has looked upon it, the most fortunate human existence must seem a disappointment.

So I, too, with the rest of the world, was following in the wake of the magical music. The lie it was drawing me by is perhaps Spring's oldest, commonest lie, — the lying promise of the Perfect Woman, the Quite

Impossible She.   Who has not dreamed of
her, — who that can dream at all?   I suppose that the dreams of our modern youth
are entirely commercial.   In the morning of
life they are rapt by intoxicating visions of
some great haberdashery business, beckoned
to by the voluptuous enticements of the
legal profession, or maybe the Holy Grail
they forswear all else to seek is a snug edi-
torial chair.   These quests and dreams were
not for me.   Since I was man I have had
but one dream, — namely, Woman.   Alas!
till this my thirtieth year I have found only
women.   No! that is disloyal, disloyal to
my First Love; for this is sadly true, —
that we always find the Golden Girl in our
first love, and lose her in our second.

I wonder if the reader would care to hear
about my First Love, of whom I am naturally
thinking a good deal this morning, under
the demoralising influences of the fresh air,
blue sky, and various birds and flowers.
More potent intoxicants these than any that
need licenses for their purveyance, respon-
sible — see the poets — for no end of human
foolishness.

I was about to tell the story of my First Love, but on second thoughts I decide not. It will keep, and I feel hungry, and yonder seems a dingle where I can lie and open my knapsack, eat, drink, and doze among the sun-flecked shadows.

CHAPTER IV

IN WHICH I EAT AND DREAM

THE girl we go to meet is the girl we have met before. I evolved this sage reflection, as, lost deep down in the green alleys of the dingle, having fortified the romantic side of my nature with sandwiches and sherry, I lazily put the question to myself as to what manner of girl I expected the Golden Girl to be. A man who goes seeking should have some notion of what he goes out to seek. Had I any ideal by which to test and measure the damsels of the world who were to pass before my critical choosing eye? Had I ever met any girl in the past who would serve approximately as a model, — any girl, in fact, I would very much like to meet again? I was very sleepy, and while trying to make up my mind I fell asleep; and lo!

the sandwiches and sherry brought me a dream that I could not but consider of good omen.   And this was the dream.

I thought my quest had brought me into a strange old haunted forest, and that I had thrown myself down to rest at the gnarled mossy root of a great oak-tree, while all about me was nought but fantastic shapes and capricious groups of gold-green bole and bough, wondrous alleys ending in mysterious coverts, and green lanes of exquisite turf that seemed to have been laid down in expectation of some milk-white queen or goddess passing that way.   And so still the forest was you could have heard an acorn drop or a bird call from one end of it to the other.   The exquisite silence was evidently waiting for the exquisite voice, that presently not so much broke as mingled with it, like a swan swimming through a lake.

"Whom seek you?" said, or rather sung, a planetary voice right at my shoulder.   But three short unmusical Saxon words, yet it was as though a mystical strain of music had passed through the wood.

"Whom seek you?" and again the lovely

speech flowered upon the silence, as white water-lilies on the surface of some shaded pool.

"The Golden Girl," I answered simply, turning my head, and looking half sideways and half upwards; and behold! the tree at whose foot I lay had opened its rocky side, and in the cleft, like a long lily-bud sliding from its green sheath, stood a dryad, and my speech failed and my breath went as I looked upon her beauty, for which mortality has no simile. Yet was there something about her of the earth-sweetness that clings even to the loveliest, star-ambitious, earth-born thing. She was not all immortal, as man is not all mortal. She was the sweetness of the strength of the oak, the soul born of the sun kissing its green leaves in the still Memnonian mornings, of moon and stars kissing its green leaves in the still Trophonian nights.

"The maid you seek," said she, and again she broke the silence like the moon breaking through the clouds, "what manner of maid is she? For a maid abides in this wood, maybe it is she whom you seek. Is

she but a lovely face you seek? Is she
but a lofty mind? Is she but a beautiful
soul?"

"Maybe she is all these, though no one
only, and more besides," I answered.

"It is well," she replied, "but have you
in your heart no image of her you seek?
Else how should you know her should you
some day come to meet her?"

"I have no image of her," I said. "I
cannot picture her; but I shall know her,
know her inerrably as these your wood children find out each other untaught, as the
butterfly that has never seen his kindred
knows his painted mate, passing on the
wing all others by. Only when the lark
shall mate with the nightingale, and the
honey-bee and the clock-beetle keep house
together, shall I wed another maid. Fair
maybe she will not be, though fair to me.
Wise maybe she will not be, though wise to
me. For riches I care not, and of her kindred
I have no care. All I know is that just to
sit by her will be bliss, just to touch her
bliss, just to hear her speak bliss beyond all
mortal telling."

Thereat the Sweetness of the Strength of the Oak smiled upon me and said, —

"Follow yonder green path till it leads you into a little grassy glade, where is a crystal well and a hut of woven boughs hard by, and you shall see her whom you seek."

And as she spoke she faded suddenly, and the side of the oak was once more as the solid rock. With hot heart I took the green winding path, and presently came the little grassy glade, and the bubbling crystal well, and the hut of wattled boughs, and, looking through the open door of the hut, I saw a lovely girl lying asleep in her golden hair. She smiled sweetly in her sleep, and stretched out her arms softly, as though to enfold the dear head of her lover. And, ere I knew, I was bending over her, and as her sweet breath came and went I whispered: "Grace o' God, I am here. I have sought you through the world, and found you at last. Grace o' God, I have come."

And then I thought her great eyes opened, as when the sun sweeps clear blue spaces in the morning sky. "Flower o' Men," then said she, low and sweet, — "Flower o' Men,

is it you indeed? As you have sought, so
have I waited, waited . . . " And thereat
her arms stole round my neck, and I awoke,
and Grace o' God was suddenly no more
than a pretty name that my dream had given
me.

"A pretty dream," said my soul, "though
a little boyish for thirty." "And a most
excellent sherry," added my body.

CHAPTER V

CONCERNING THE PERFECT WOMAN, AND
THEREFORE CONCERNING ALL FEMININE
READERS

As I once more got under way, my thoughts
slowly loitered back to the theme which had
been occupying them before I dropped
asleep. What was my working hypothesis
of the Perfect Woman, towards whom I was
thus leisurely strolling? She might be
defined, I reflected, as The Woman Who Is
Worthy Of Us; but the improbability which
every healthily conceited young man must
feel of ever finding such a one made the
definition seem a little unserviceable. Or,
if you prefer, since we seem to be dealing
with impossibles, we might turn about and
more truly define her as The Woman of
Whom We are Worthy, for who dare say that
she exists? If, again, she were defined as the

Woman our More Fortunate Friend Marries, her unapproachableness would rob the definition of any practical value. Other generalisations proving equally unprofitable, I began scientifically to consider in detail the attributes of the supposititious paragon, —attributes of body and mind and heart. This was soon done; but again, as I thus conned all those virtues which I was to expect united in one unhappy woman, the result was still unsatisfying, for I began to perceive that it was really not perfection that I was in search of. As I added virtue after virtue to the female monster in my mind, and the result remained still inanimate and unalluring, I realised that the lack I was conscious of was not any new perfection, but just one or two honest human imperfections. And this, try as I would, was just what I could not imagine.

For, if you reflect a moment, you will see that, while it is easy to choose what virtues we would have our wife possess, it is all but impossible to imagine those faults we would desire in her, which I think most lovers would admit add piquancy to the loved one,

that fascinating wayward imperfection which
paradoxically makes her perfect.

Faults in the abstract are each and all so
uninviting, not to say alarming, but, asso-
ciated with certain eyes and hair and tender
little gowns, it is curious how they lose
their terrors; and, as with vice in the poet's
image, we end by embracing what we began
by dreading. You see the fault becomes a
virtue when it is hers, the treason prospers;
wherefore, no doubt, the impossibility of
imagining it. What particular fault will suit
a particular unknown girl is obviously as
difficult to determine as in what colours she
will look her best.

So, I say, I plied my brains in vain for
that becoming fault. It was the same
whether I considered her beauty, her heart,
or her mind. A charming old Italian writer
has laid down the canons of perfect feminine
beauty with much nicety in a delicious discourse, which, as he delivered it in a sixteenth-
century Florentine garden to an audience of
beautiful and noble ladies, an audience not
too large to be intimate and not too small
to be embarrassing, it was his delightful

good fortune and privilege to illustrate by pretty and sly references to the characteristic beauties of the several ladies seated like a ring of roses around him.   Thus he would refer to the shape of Madonna Lampiada's sumptuous eyelids, and to her shell-like ears, to the correct length and shape of Madonna Amororrisca's nose, to the lily tower of Madonna Verdespina's throat; nor would the unabashed old Florentine shrink from calling attention to the unfairness of Madonna Selvaggia's covering up her dainty bosom, just as he was about to discourse upon "those two hills of snow and of roses with two little crowns of fine rubies on their peaks."   How could a man lecture if his diagrams were going to behave like that! Then, feigning a tiff, he would close his manuscript, and all the ladies with their birdlike voices would beseech him with "Oh, no, Messer Firenzuola, please go on again; it's *so* charming!" while, as if by accident, Madonna Selvaggia's moonlike bosom would once more slip out its heavenly silver, perceiving which, Messer Firenzuola would open his manuscript again and pro· ceed with his sweet learning.

Happy Firenzuola! Oh, days that are
no more!

By selecting for his illustrations one
feature from one lady and another from
another, Messer Firenzuola builds up an
ideal of the Beautiful Woman, which, were
she to be possible, would probably be as
faultily faultless as the Perfect Woman,
were she possible.   Moreover, much about
the same time as Firenzuola was writing,
Botticelli's blonde, angular, *retroussé* women
were breaking every one of that beauty-
master's canons, perfect in beauty none the
less; and lovers then, and perhaps particularly now, have found the perfect beauty in
faces to which Messer Firenzuola would
have denied the name of face at all, by
virtue of a quality which indeed he has
tabulated, but which is far too elusive and
undefinable, too spiritual for him truly to have
understood, — a quality which nowadays we
are tardily recognising as the first and last
of all beauty, either of nature or art, — the
supreme, truly divine, because material-
istically unaccountable, quality of Charm!

> " Beauty that makes holy earth and heaven
> May have faults from head to feet."

O loveliest and best-loved face that ever hallowed the eyes that now seek for you in vain! Such was your strange lunar magic, such the light not even death could dim. And such may be the loveliest and best-loved face for you who are reading these pages, — faces little understood on earth because they belong to heaven.

There is indeed only one law of beauty on which we may rely, — that it invariably breaks all the laws laid down for it by the professors of æsthetics. All the beauty that has ever been in the world has broken the laws of all previous beauty, and unwillingly dictated laws to the beauty that succeeded it, — laws which that beauty has no less spiritedly broken, to prove in turn dictator to its successor.

The immortal sculptors, painters, and poets have always done exactly what their critics forbade them to do. The obedient in art are always the forgotten.

Likewise beautiful women have always been a law unto themselves. Who could have prophesied in what way any of these inspired law-breakers would break the law, what new type of perfect imperfection they would create?

So we return to the Perfect Woman, having gained this much knowledge of her, — that her perfection is nothing more or less than her unique, individual, charming imperfection, and that she is simply the woman we love and who is fool enough to love us.

CHAPTER VI

IN WHICH THE AUTHOR ANTICIPATES DIS-
CONTENT ON THE PART OF HIS READER

"BUT come," I imagine some reader com-
plaining, "isn't it high time for something
to happen?" No doubt it is, but what am I
to do? I am no less discontented. Is it not
even more to my interest than to the reader's
for something to happen? Here have I been
tramping along since breakfast-time, and
now it is late in the afternoon, but never a
feather of her dove's wings, never a flutter
of her angel's robes have I seen. It is dis-
heartening, for one naturally expects to find
anything we seek a few minutes after starting out to seek it, and I confess that I
expected to find my golden mistress within
a very few hours of leaving home. However, had that been the case, there would

have been no story, as the novelists say, and I trust, as he goes on, the reader may feel with me that that would have been a pity. Besides, with that prevision given to an author, I am strongly of opinion that something will happen before long. And if the worst comes to the worst, there is always that story of my First Love wherewith to fill the time. Meanwhile I am approaching a decorative old Surrey town, little more than a cluster of ripe old inns, to one of which I have much pleasure in inviting the reader to dinner.

CHAPTER VII

PRANDIAL

DINNER!

Is there a more beautiful word in the language?

Dinner!

Let the beautiful word come as a refrain to and fro this chapter.

Dinner!

Just eating and drinking, nothing more, but so much!

Drinking, indeed, has had its laureates. Yet would I offer my mite of prose in its honour. And when I say "drinking," I speak not of smuggled gin or of brandy bottles held fiercely by the neck till they are empty.

Nay, but of that lonely glass in the social solitude of the tavern, — alone, but not alone, for the glass is sure to bring a dream to bear it company, and it is a poor dream

that cannot raise a song.   And what greater
felicity than to be alone in a tavern with
your last new song, just born and yet still
a tingling part of you.

Drinking has indeed been sung, but why,
I have heard it asked, have we no " Eating
Songs?" — for eating is, surely, a fine pleasure.   Many practise it already, and it is becoming more general every day.

I speak not of the finicking joy of the
gourmet, but the joy of an honest appetite
in ecstasy, the elemental joy of absorbing
quantities of fresh simple food, — mere roast
lamb, new potatoes, and peas of living green.

It is, indeed, an absorbing pleasure.   It
needs all our attention.   You must eat as
you kiss, so exacting are the joys of the
mouth, — talking, for example.   The quiet
eye may be allowed to participate, and sometimes the ear, where the music is played
upon a violin, and that a Stradivarius.   A
well-kept lawn, with six-hundred-years-old
cedars and a twenty-feet yew hedge, will add
distinction to the meal.   Nor should one
ever eat without a seventeenth-century poet
in an old yellow-leaved edition upon the

table, not to be read, of course, any more
than the flowers are to be eaten, but just to
make music of association very softly to our
thoughts.

Some diners have wine too upon the table,
and in the pauses of thinking what a divine
mystery dinner is, they eat.

For dinner *is* a mystery, — a mystery of
which even the greatest *chef* knows but
little, as a poet knows not,

> " with all his lore,
> Wherefore he sang, or whence the mandate sped."

"Even our digestion is governed by
angels," said Blake; and if you will resist
the trivial inclination to substitute "bad
angels," is there really any greater mystery
than the process by which beef is turned
into brains, and beer into beauty? Every
beautiful woman we see has been made out
of beefsteaks. It is a solemn thought, — and
the finest poem that was ever written came
out of a grey pulpy mass such as we make
brain sauce of.

And with these grave thoughts for grace
let us sit down to dinner.

Dinner!

CHAPTER VIII

STILL PRANDIAL

WHAT wine shall we have? I confess I am no judge of wines, except when they are bad. To-night I feel inclined to allow my choice to be directed by sentiment; and as we are on so pretty a pilgrimage, would it not be appropriate to drink Liebfraumilch?

Hock is full of fancy, and all wines are by their very nature full of reminiscence, the golden tears and red blood of summers that are gone.

Forgive me, therefore, if I grow reminiscent. Indeed, I fear that the hour for the story of my First Love has come. But first, notice the waitress. I confess, whether beautiful or plain, — not too plain, — women who earn their own living have a peculiar attraction for me.

I hope the Golden Girl will not turn out to be a duchess.   As old Campion sings, —

> " I care not for those ladies
>   Who must be wooed and prayed;
> Give me kind Amaryllis,
>   The wanton country-maid."

Town-maids too of the same pattern. Whether in town or country, give me the girls that work. The Girls That Work! But evidently it is high time we began a new chapter.

CHAPTER IX

THE LEGEND OF HEBE, OR THE HEAVENLY HOUSEMAID

YES, I blush to admit it, my First Love was a housemaid. So was she known on this dull earth of ours, but in heaven — in the heaven of my imagination, at all events — she was, of course, a goddess. How she managed to keep her disguise I never could understand. To me she was so obviously *dea certe*. The nimbus was so apparent. Yet no one seemed to see it but me. I have heard her scolded as though she were any ordinary earthly housemaid, and I have seen the butcher's boy trying to flirt with her without a touch of reverence.

Maybe I understood because I saw her in that early hour of the morning when even the stony Memnon sings, in that mystical light of the young day when divine exiled things, condemned to rough bondage through the noon, are for a short magical hour their own celestial selves, their unearthly glory as yet unhidden by any earthly disguise.

Neither fairies nor fauns, dryads nor nymphs of the forest pools, have really passed away from the world. You have only to get up early enough to meet them in the meadows. They rarely venture abroad after six. All day long they hide in uncouth enchanted forms. They change maybe to a field of turnips, and I have seen a farmer priding himself on a flock of sheep that I knew were really a most merry company of dryads and fauns in disguise. I had but to make the sign of the cross, sprinkle some holy water upon them, and call them by their sweet secret names, and the whole rout had been off to the woods, with mad gambol and song, before the eyes of the astonished farmer.

It was so with Hebe. She was really a little gold-haired blue-eyed dryad, whose true home was a wild white cherry-tree that grew in some scattered woodland behind the

3

old country-house of my boyhood. In spring-
time how that naughty tree used to flash its
silver nakedness of blossom for miles across
the furze and scattered birches!

I might have known it was Hebe.

Alas! it no longer bares its bosom with
so dazzling a prodigality, for it is many a
day since it was uprooted. The little dryad
long since fled away weeping, — fled away,
said evil tongues, fled away to the town.

Well do I remember our last meeting.
Returning home one evening, I met her at
the lodge-gate hurrying away. Our loves
had been discovered, and my mother had
shuddered to think that so pagan a thing
had lived so long in a Christian house. I
vowed — ah! what did I not vow? — and then
we stole sadly together to comfort our aching
hearts under cover of the woodland. For
the last time the wild cherry-tree bloomed,
— wonderful blossom, glittering with tears,
and gloriously radiant with stormy lights of
wild passion and wilder hopes.

My faith lived valiantly till the next
spring. It was Hebe who was faithless.
The cherry-tree was dead, for its dryad had

gone, — fled, said evil tongues, fled away to the town!

But as yet, in the time to which my thoughts return, our sweet secret mornings were known only to ourselves. It was my custom then to rise early, to read Latin authors, — thanks to Hebe, still unread. I used to light my fire and make tea for myself, till one rapturous morning I discovered that Hebe was fond of rising early too, and that she would like to light my fire and make my tea. After a time she began to sweeten it for me. And then she would sit on my knee, and we would translate Catullus together, — into English kisses; for she was curiously interested in the learned tongue.

How lovely she used to look with the morning sun turning her hair to golden mist, and dancing in the blue deeps of her eyes; and once when by chance she had forgotten to fasten her gown, I caught glimpses of a bosom that was like two happy handfuls of wonderful white cherries . . .

She wore a marvellous little printed gown. And here I may say that I have never to this day understood objections which were afterwards raised against my early attachment to print. The only legitimate attachment to print stuff, I was told, was to print stuff in the form of blouse, tennis, or boating costume. Yet, thought I, I would rather smuggle one of those little print gowns into my berth than all the silks a sea-faring friend of mine takes the trouble to smuggle from far Cathay. However, every one to his taste; for me,

> No silken madam, by your leave,
> 　Though wondrous, wondrous she be,
> Can lure this heart — upon my sleeve —
> 　From little pink-print Hebe.

For I found beneath that pretty print such a heart as seldom beats beneath your satin, warm and wild as a bird's. I used to put my ear to it sometimes to listen if it beat right. Ah, reader, it was like putting your ear to the gate of heaven.

And once I made a song for her, which ran like this: —

> There grew twin apples high on a bough
> 　Within an orchard fair ;
> The tree was all of gold, I vow,
> 　And the apples of silver were.

And whoso kisseth those apples high,
Who kisseth once is a king,
Who kisseth twice shall never die,
Who kisseth thrice — oh, were it I ! —
May ask for anything.

Hebe blushed, and for answer whispered something too sweet to tell.

"Dear little head sunning over with curls," were I to meet you now, what would happen? Ah! to meet you now were too painfully to measure the remnant of my youth.

CHAPTER X

AGAIN ON FOOT — THE GIRLS THAT NEVER CAN BE MINE

NEXT morning I was afoot early, bent on my quest in right good earnest; for I had a remorseful feeling that I had not been sufficiently diligent the day before, had spent too much time in dreaming and moralising, in which opinion I am afraid the reader will agree.

So I was up and out of the town while as yet most of the inhabitants were in the throes of getting up. Somewhere too *She*, the Golden One, the White Woman, was drowsily tossing the night-clothes from her limbs and rubbing her sleepy eyes. William Morris's lovely song came into my mind, —

> " And midst them all, perchance, my love
> Is waking, and doth gently move
> And stretch her soft arms out to me,
> Forgetting thousand leagues of sea."

Perhaps she was in the very town I was leaving behind. Perhaps we had slept within a few houses of each other. Who could tell?

Looking back at the old town, with its one steep street climbing the white face of the chalk hill, I remembered what wonderful exotic women Thomas Hardy had found eating their hearts out behind the windows of dull country high streets, through which hung waving no banners of romance, outwardly as unpromising of adventure as the windows of the town I had left. And then turning my steps across a wide common, which ran with gorse and whortleberry bushes away on every side to distant hilly horizons, swarthy with pines, and dotted here and there with stone granges and white villages, I thought of all the women within that circle, any one of whom might prove the woman I sought, — from milkmaids crossing the meadows, their strong shoulders straining with the weight of heavy pails, to fine ladies dying of *ennui* in their country-houses; pretty farmers' daughters surreptitiously reading novels, and longing for London and "life;" passionate young farmers' wives already weary of their doltish lords; bright-eyed bar-maids buried alive in country inns, and wondering "whatever possessed them" to leave Manchester, — for bar-maids seem always to come from Manchester, — all long-ing modestly, said I, to set eyes on a man like me, a man of romance, a man of feeling, a man, if you like, to run away with.

My heart flooded over with tender pity for these poor sweet women — though perhaps chiefly for my own sad lot in not encounter-ing them, — and I conceived a great compre-hensive love-poem to be entitled "The Girls that never can be Mine." Perhaps before the end of our tramp together, I shall have a few verses of it to submit to the elegant taste of the reader, but at present I have not advanced beyond the title.

CHAPTER XI

AN OLD MAN OF THE HILLS, AND THE SCHOOLMASTER'S STORY

WHILE occupying myself with these no doubt wanton reflections on the unfair division of opportunities in human life, I was leisurely crossing the common, and presently I came up with a pedestrian who, though I had little suspected it as I caught sight of him ahead, was destined by a kind providence to make more entertaining talk for me in half an hour than most people provide in a lifetime.

He was an oldish man, turned sixty, one would say, and belonging, to judge from his dress and general appearance, to what one might call the upper labouring class. He wore a decent square felt hat, a shabby respectable overcoat, a workman's knitted waistcoat, and workman's corduroys, and he carried an umbrella. His upper part might have belonged to a small well-to-do trades-man, while his lower bore marks of recent bricklaying. Without its being remarkable, he had what one calls a good face, somewhat aquiline in character, with a refined fore-head and nose. His cheeks were shaved, and his whitening beard and moustache were worn somewhat after the fashion of Charles Dickens. This gave a slight touch of severity to a face that was full of quiet strength.

Passing the time of day to each other, we were soon in conversation, I asking him this and that question about the neighbouring country-side, of which I gathered he was an old inhabitant.

"Yes," he said presently, "I was the first to put stick or stone on Whortleberry Common yonder. Fifteen years ago I built my own wood cottage there, and now I'm rebuilding it of good Surrey stone."

"Do you mean that you are building it yourself, with your own hands, no one to help you?" I asked.

"Not so much as to carry a pail of water,"

he replied. "I'm my own contractor, my own carpenter, and my own bricklayer, and I shall be sixty-seven come Michaelmas," he added, by no means irrelevantly.

There was pride in his voice, — pardonable pride, I thought, for who of us would not be proud to be able to build his own house from floor to chimney?

"Sixty-seven, — a man can see and do a good deal in that time," I said, not flattering myself on the originality of the remark, but desiring to set him talking. In the country, as elsewhere, we must forego profundity if we wish to be understood.

"Yes, sir," he said, "I have been about a good deal in my time. I have seen pretty well all of the world there is to see, and sailed as far as ship could take me."

"Indeed, you have been a sailor too?"

"Twenty-two thousand miles of sea," he continued, without directly answering my remark. "Yes, Vancouver's about as far as any vessel need want to go; and then I have caught seals off the coast of Labrador, and walked my way through the raspberry plains at the back of the White Mountains."

"Vancouver," "Labrador," "The White Mountains," the very names, thus casually mentioned on a Surrey heath, seemed full of the sounding sea. Like talismans they whisked one away to strange lands, across vast distances of space imagination refused to span. Strange to think that the shabby little man at my side had them all fast locked, pictures upon pictures, in his brain, and as we were talking was back again in goodness knows what remote latitude.

I kept looking at him and saying, "Twenty-two thousand miles of sea! sixty-seven! and builds his own cottage!"

In addition to all this he had found time to be twenty-one years a policeman, and to beget and rear successfully twelve children. He was now, I gathered, living partly on his pension, and spoke of this daughter married, this daughter in service here, and that daughter in service there, one son settled in London and another in the States, with something of a patriarchal pride, with the independent air too of a man who could honestly say to himself that, with few advantages from fortune, having had, so to say, to work his passage, every foot and hour of it, across those twenty-two thousand miles and those sixty-seven years, he had made a thoroughly creditable job of his life.

As we walked along I caught glimpses in his vivid and ever-varying talk of the qualities that had made his success possible. They are always the same qualities!

A little pile of half-hewn stones, the remains of a ruined wall, scattered by the roadside caught his eye.

"I 've seen the time when I would n't have left them stones lying out there," he said, and presently, "Why, God bless you, I 've made my own boots before to-day.   Give me the tops and I 'll soon rig up a pair still."

And with all his success, and his evident satisfaction with his lot, the man was neither a prig nor a teetotaller.   He had probably seen too much of the world to be either.   Yet he had, he said, been too busy all his life to spend much time in public-houses, as we drank a pint of ale together in the inn which stood at the end of the common.

"No, it 's all well enough in its way, but

it swallows time," he remarked. "You see, my wife and I have our own pin at home, and when I'm a bit tired, I just draw a glass for myself, and smoke a pipe, and there's no time wasted coming and going, and drinking first with this and then with the other."

A little way past the inn we came upon a notice-board whereon the lord of the manor warned all wayfarers against trespassing on the common by making encampments, lighting fires or cutting firewood thereon, and to this fortunate circumstance I owe the most interesting story my companion had to tell.

We had mentioned the lord of the manor as we crossed the common, and the notice-board brought him once more to the old man's mind.

"Poor gentleman!" he said, pointing to the board as though it was the lord of the manor himself standing there, "I should n't like to have had the trouble he's had on my shoulders."

"Indeed?" I said interrogatively.

"Well, you see, sir," he continued, instinctively lowering his voice to a confidential impressiveness, "he married an

actress; a noble lady too she was, a fine
dashing merry lady as ever you saw.   All
went well for a time, and then it suddenly
got whispered about that she and the village
schoolmaster were meeting each other at
nights, in the meadow-bottom at the end of
her own park.   It lies over that way, — I
could take you to the very place.   The
schoolmaster was a noble-looking young
man too, a devil-me-care blade of a fellow,
with a turn for poetry, they said, and a
merry man too, and much in request for
a song at The Moonrakers of an evening.
Many's the night I've heard the windows
rattling with the good company gathered
round him.   Yes, he was a noble-looking
man, a noble-looking man," he repeated
wistfully, and with an evident sympathy
for the lovers which, I need hardly say,
won my heart.

"But how, I wonder, did they come to
know each other?" I interrupted, anxious
to learn all I could, even if I had to ask
stupid questions to learn it.

"Well, of course, no one can say how
these things come about.   She was the lady

of the manor and the patroness of his school;
and then, as I say, he was a very noble-
looking man, and probably took her fancy;
and, sir, whenever some women set their
hearts on a man there's no stopping them.
Have him they will, whatever happens.
They can't help it, poor things! It's just
a freak of nature."

"Well, and how was it found out?" I
again jogged him.

"One of Sir William's keepers played the
spy on them. He spread it all over the
place how he had seen them on moonlight
nights sitting together in the dingle, drinking champagne, and laughing and talking as
merry as you please; and, of course, it came
in time to Sir William — "

"You see that green lane there," he broke
off, pointing to a romantic path winding
along the heath side; "it was along there he
used to go of a night to meet her after every
one was in bed; and when it all came out
there was a regular cartload of bottles found
there. The squire had them all broken up,
but the pieces are there to this day.

"Yes," he again proceeded, "it hit Sir

William very hard. He's never been the same man since."

I am afraid that my sympathies were less with Sir William than better regulated sympathies would have been. I confess that my imagination was more occupied with that picture of the two lovers making merry together in the moonlit dingle.

Is it not, indeed, a fascinating little story, with its piquant contrasts and its wild love-at-all-costs? And how many such stories are hidden about the country, lying carelessly in rustic memories, if one only knew where to find them!

At this point my companion left me, and I — well, I confess that I retraced my steps to the common and rambled up that green lane, along which the romantic schoolmaster used to steal in the moonlight to the warm arms of his love. How eagerly he had trodden the very turf I was treading, — we never know at what moment we are treading sacred earth! But for that old man, I had passed along this path without a thrill. Had I not but an hour ago stood upon this very common, vainly, so it seemed, invoking the

4

spirits of passion and romance, and the grim old common had never made a sign. And now I stood in the very dingle where they had so often and so wildly met; and it was all gone, quite gone away for ever. The hours that had seemed so real, the kisses that had seemed like to last for ever, the vows, the tears, all now as if they had never been, gone on the four winds, lost in the abysses of time and space.

And to think of all the thousands and thousands of lovers who had loved no less wildly and tenderly, made sweet these lanes with their vows, made green these meadows with their feet; and they, too, all gone, their bright eyes fallen to dust, their sweet voices for ever put to silence.

To which I would add, for the benefit of the profane, that I sought in vain for those broken bottles.

CHAPTER XII

THE TRUTH ABOUT THE GIPSIES

I FELT lonely after losing my companion, and I met nobody to take his place. In fact, for a couple of hours I met nothing worth mentioning, male or female, with the exception of a gipsy caravan, which I suppose was both; but it was a poor show. Borrow would have blushed for it. In fact, it is my humble opinion that the gipsies have been overdone, just as the Alps have been over-climbed. I have no great desire to see Switzerland, for I am sure the Alps must be greasy with being climbed.

Besides, the Alps and the gipsies, in common with waterfalls and ruined castles, belong to the ready-made operatic poetry of the world, from which the last thrill has long since departed. They are, so to say, public poetry, the public property of the emotions, and no longer touch the private heart or stir the private imagination. Our fathers felt so much about them that there is nothing left for us to feel. They are as a rose whose fragrance has been exhausted by greedy and indiscriminate smelling. I would rather find a little Surrey common for myself and idle about it a summer day, with the other geese and donkeys, than climb the tallest Alp.

Most gipsies are merely tenth-rate provincial companies, travelling with and villainously travestying Borrow's great pieces of "Lavengro" and "Romany Rye." Dirty, ill-looking, scowling men; dirty, slovenly, and wickedly ugly women; children to match, snarling, filthy little curs, with a ready beggar's whine on occasion. A gipsy encampment to-day is little more than a moving slum, a scab of squalor on the fair face of the countryside.

But there was one little trifle of an incident that touched me as I passed this particular caravan. Evidently one of the vans had come to grief, and several men of the

party were making a great show of repairing
it.   After I had run the gauntlet of the
begging children, and was just out of ear-
shot of the group, I turned round to survey
it from a distance.   It was encamped on a
slight rise of the undulating road, and from
where I stood tents and vans and men were
clearly silhouetted against the sky.   The
road ran through and a little higher than
the encampment, which occupied both sides
of it.   Presently the figure of a young man
separated itself from the rest, stept up on to
the smooth road, and standing in the middle
of it, in an absorbed attitude, began to make
a movement with his hands as though winding string round a top.   That in fact was his
occupation, and for the next five minutes he
kept thus winding the cord, flinging the top
to the ground, and intently bending down
to catch it on his hand, none of the others,
not even the children, taking the slightest
notice of him, — he entirely alone there with
his poor little pleasure.   There seemed to
me pathos in his loneliness.   Had some one
spun the top with him, it would have
vanished; and presently, no doubt at the

bidding of an oath I could not hear, he
hurriedly thrust the top into his pocket, and
once more joined the straining group of
men.   The snatched pleasure must be put
by at the call of reality; the world and its
work must rush in upon his dream.   I have
often thought about the top and its spinner,
as I have noted the absorbed faces of other
people's pleasures in the streets, — two
lovers passing along the crowded Strand
with eyes only for each other; a student
deep in his book in the corner of an omni-
bus; a young mother glowing over the child
in her arms; the wild-eyed musician dreamily
treading on everybody's toes, and begging
nobody's pardon; the pretty little Gaiety
Girl hurrying to rehearsal with no thought
but of her own sweet self and whether there
will be a letter from Harry at the stage-
door, — yes, if we are alone in our griefs, we
are no less alone in our pleasures.   We spin
our tops as in an enchanted circle, and no
one sees or heeds save ourselves, — as how
should they with their own tops to spin?
Happy indeed is he who has his top and
cares still to spin it; for to be tired of our

tops is to be tired of life, saith the preacher.

As the young gipsy's little holiday came to an end, I turned with a sigh upon my way; and here, while still on the subject, may I remark on the curious fact that probably Borrow has lived and died without a single gipsy having heard of him, just as the expertest anglers know nothing of Izaak Walton.

Has the British soldier, one wonders, yet discovered Rudyard Kipling, or is the Wessex peasant aware of Thomas Hardy? It is odd to think that the last people to read such authors are the very people they most concern. For you might spend your life, say, in studying the London street boy, and write never so movingly and humourously about him, yet would he never know your name; and though Whitechapel makes novelists, it does so without knowing it, — makes them to be read in Mayfair, — just as it never wears the dainty hats and gowns its weary little milliners and seamstresses make through the day and night. It is Capital and Labour over again, for in literature also we reap in gladness what others have sown in tears.

And now, after these admirable reflections, I am about to make such "art" as I can of another man's tragedy, as will appear in the next chapter.

CHAPTER XIII

A STRANGE WEDDING

MY moralisings were cut short by my entering a village, and, it being about the hour of noon, finding myself in the thick of a village wedding.

Undoubtedly the nicest way to get married is on the sly, and indeed it is at present becoming quite fashionable. Many young couples of my acquaintance, who have had no other reason for concealing the fact beyond their own whim, have thus slipped off without saying a word to anybody, and returned full-blown housekeepers, with "at home" days of their own, and everything else like real married people, — for, as said an old lady to me, "one can never be sure of married people nowadays unless you have been at the wedding."

My friend George Muncaster, who does
everything charmingly different from any
one else, hit upon one of the quaintest plans
for his marriage.   It was simple, and some
may say prosaic enough.   His days being
spent at a great office in the city, he got
leave of absence for a couple of hours, met
his wife, went with her to the registrar's,
returned to his office, worked the rest of the
day as usual, and then went to his new home
to find his wife and dinner awaiting him, —
all just as it was going to be every night
for so many happy years.   Prosaic, you say!
Not your idea of poetry, perhaps, but, after
a new and growing fashion in poetry, truly
poetic.   George Muncaster's marriage is a
type of the new poetry, the poetry of essen-
tials.   The old poetry, as exemplified in the
old-fashioned marriage, is a poetry of exter-
nals, and certainly it has the advantage of
picturesqueness.

There is perhaps more to be said for it
than that.   Indeed, if I were ever to get
married, I am at a loss to know which way I
should choose, — George Muncaster's way or
the old merry fashion, with the rice and the

old shoes and the orange-blossom. No
doubt the old cheery publicity is a little
embarrassing to the two most concerned, and
the old marriage customs, the singing of the
bride and bridegroom to their nuptial couch,
the frank jests, the country horse-play, must
have fretted the souls of many a lover before
Shelley, who, it will be remembered, resented
the choral celebrations of his Scotch landlord and friends by appearing at his bedroom
door with a brace of pistols.

How like Shelley! The Scotch landlord
meant well, we may be sure, and a very
small pinch of humour, or even mere ordinary humanity, as distinct from humanitarianism, would have taken in the situation.
Of course Shelley's mind was full of the
sanctity of the moment, and indignant that
"the hour for which the years did sigh"
should thus be broken in upon by vulgar
revelry; but while we may sympathise with
his view, and admit to the full the sacred-
ness, not to say the solemnity, of the marriage ceremony, yet it is to be hoped that it
still retains a naturally mirthful side, of
which such public merriment is but the

crude expression. With all its sweet and mystical significance, surely the prevailing feeling in the hearts of bride and bridegroom is, or should be, that of happiness, — happiness bubbling and dancing, all sunny ripples from heart to heart.

Surely they can spare a little of it, just one day's sight of it, to a less happy world, — a world long since married and done for, and with little happiness in it save the spectacle of other people's happiness. It is good for us to see happy people, good for the symbols of happiness to be carried high amidst us on occasion; for if they serve no other purpose, they inspire in us the hope that we too may some day be happy, or remind our discontented hearts that we have been.

If it were only for the sake of those quaint old women for whom life would be entirely robbed of interest were it not for other people's weddings and funerals, one feels the public ceremony of marriage a sort of public duty, the happiness tax, so to say, due to the somewhat impoverished revenues of public happiness. Other forms of happiness are taxed; why not marriage?

In a village, particularly, two people who robbed the community of its perquisites in this respect would be looked upon as "enemies of the people," and their joint life would begin under a social ban which it would cost much subsequent hospitality to remove. The dramatic instinct to which the life of towns is necessarily unfavourable, is kept alive in the country by the smallness of the stage and the fewness of the actors. A village is an organism, conscious of its several parts, as a town is not. In a village everybody is a public man. The great events of his life are of public as well as private significance, appropriately, therefore, invested with public ceremonial. Thus used to living in the public eye, the actors carry off their parts at weddings and other dramatic ceremonials, with more spirit than is easy to a townsman, who is naturally made self-conscious by being suddenly called upon to fill for a day a public position for which he has had no training. That no doubt is the real reason for the growth of quiet marriages; and the desire for them, I suspect, comes first from the man, for there are few women who at heart do not prefer the old histrionic display.

However, the village wedding at which I suddenly found myself a spectator was, for a village, a singularly quiet one. There was no bell-ringing, and there were no brides-maids. The bride drove up quietly with her father, and there was a subdued note even in the murmur of recognition which ran along the villagers as they stood in groups near the church porch. There was an absence of the usual hilarity which struck me. One might almost have said that there was a quite ominous silence.

Seating myself in a corner of the transept where I could see all and be little seen, I with the rest awaited the coming of the overdue bridegroom. Meanwhile the usual buzzing and bobbing of heads went on amongst the usual little group near the foot of the altar. Now and then one caught a glisten of tears through a widow's veil, and the little bride, dressed quietly in grey, talked with the usual nervous gaiety to her girl friends, and made the usual whispered confidences about her trousseau. The father,

in occasional conversation with one and
another, appeared to be avoiding the subject
with the usual self-conscious solemnity, and
occasionally he looked, somewhat anxiously,
I thought, towards the church door.   The
bridegroom did not keep us waiting long, — I
noticed that he had a rather delicate sad
face, — and presently the service began.

I don't know myself what getting married
must feel like, but it cannot be much more
exciting than watching other people getting
married.   Probably the spectators are more
conscious of the impressive meaning of it
all than the brave young people themselves.   I say brave, for I am always struck
by the courage of the two who thus gaily
leap into the gulf of the unknown together,
thus join hands over the inevitable, and put
their signatures to the irrevocable.   Indeed,
I always get something like a palpitation of
the heart just before the priest utters those
final fateful words, " I declare you man and —
wife."   Half a second before you were still
free, half a second after you are bound for
the term of your natural life.   Half a second
before you had only to dash the book from

the priest's hands, and put your hand over
his mouth, and though thus giddily swinging on the brink of the precipice, you are
saved. Half a second after

> Not all the king's horses and all the king's men
> Can make you a bachelor ever again.

It is the knife-edge moment 'twixt time and
eternity.

And, curiously enough, while my thoughts
were thus running on towards the rapids of
that swirling moment, the very thing happened which I had often imagined might
happen to myself. Suddenly, with a sob,
the bridegroom covered his face with his
hands, and crying, "I cannot! I cannot!"
hurriedly left the church, tears streaming
down his cheeks, to the complete dismay of
the sad little group at the altar, and the
consternation of all present.

"Poor young man! I thought he would
never go through with it," said an old
woman half to herself, who was sitting near
me. I involuntarily looked my desire of
explanation.

"Well, you see," she said, "he had been

married before.   His first wife died four
years ago, and he loved her beyond all
heaven and earth."

That evening, I afterwards heard, the
young bridegroom's body was found by some
boys as they went to bathe in the river.   As
I recalled once more that sad yearning face,
and heard again that terrible "I cannot! I
cannot!" I thought of Heine's son of Asra,
who loved the Sultan's daughter.

"What is thy name, slave?" asked the
princess, "and what thy race and birth-
place?"

"My name," the young slave answered,
"is Mahomet.   I come from Yemen.   My
race is that of Asra, and when we love, we
die."

And likewise a voice kept saying in my
heart, "If ever you find your Golden Bride,
be sure she will die."

5

CHAPTER XIV

THE MYSTERIOUS PETTICOAT

THE sad thoughts with which this incident naturally left me were at length and suddenly dispersed, as sad thoughts not infrequently are, by a petticoat. When I say petticoat, I use the word in its literal sense, not colloquially as a metaphor for its usual wearer, meaning thereby a dainty feminine undergarment seen only by men on rainy days, and one might add washing-days. It was indeed to the fortunate accident of its being washing-day at the pretty cottage near which in the course of my morning wanderings I had set me down to rest, that I owed the sight of the petticoat in question.

But first allow me to describe a little more fully my surroundings at the moment. Not indeed that I can hope to put into words the

charm of those embowered cottages, like
nests in the armpits of great trees, tucked
snugly in the hollows of those narrow, winding, almost subterranean lanes which burrow
their way beneath the warm-hearted Surrey
woodlands.

Nothing can be straighter and smoother
than a Surrey road — when it is on the
king's business; then it is a high-road and
behaves accordingly: but a Surrey bye-road
is the most whimsical companion in the
world. It is like a sheep-dog, always running backwards and forwards, poking into
the most out-of-the-way corners, now climbing at a run some steep hummock of the
down, and now leisurely going miles about
to escape an ant-hill; and all the time (here,
by the way, ends the sheep-dog) it is stopping to gossip with rillets vagabond as itself,
or loitering to bedeck itself with flowers. It
seems as innocent of a destination as a boy
on an errand; but, after taking at least six
times as long as any other road in the kingdom for its amount of work, you usually find
it dip down of a sudden into some lovely
natural cul-de-sac, a meadow-bottom sur-

rounded by trees, with a stream spreading itself in fantastic silver shallows through its midst, and a cottage half hidden at the end. Had the lane been going to some great house, it would have made more haste, we may be sure.

The lane I had been following had finally dropped me down at something of a run upon just such a scene. The cottage, built substantially of grey stone, stood upon the side of the slope, and a broad strip of garden, half cultivated and half wild, began near the house with cabbages, and ended in a jungle of giant bulrushes as it touched the stream. Golden patches of ragwort blazed here and there among a tangled mass of no doubt worthier herbage, — such even in nature is the power of gold, — and there were the usual birds.

However, my business is with the week's washing, which in various shades of white, with occasional patches of scarlet, fluttered fantastically across a space of the garden, thereby giving unmistakable witness to human inhabitants, male and female.

As I lounged upon the green bank, I lazily

watched these parodies of humanity as they
were tossed hither and thither with humour-
ous indignity by the breeze, remarking to
myself on the quaint shamelessness with
which we thus expose to the public view
garments which at other times we are at such
bashful pains to conceal.   And thus philo-
sophising, like a much greater philosopher,
upon clothes, I found myself involuntarily
deducing the cottage family from the family
washing.   I soon decided that there must be
at least one woman say of the age of fifty,
one young woman, one little child, sex
doubtful, and one man probably young.
Further than this it was impossible to conjecture.   Thus I made the rough guess that
a young man and his wife, a child, and a
mother-in-law were among the inhabitants
of this idyllic cottage.

But the clothes-line presented charming
evidence of still another occupant; and here,
though so far easy to read, came in something of a puzzle.   Who in this humble out-
of-the-way cottage could afford to wear that
exquisite cambric petticoat edged with a fine
and very expensive lace?   And surely it was

on no country legs that those delicately
clocked and open-worked silk stockings
walked invisible through the world.

Nor was the lace any ordinary expensive
English lace, such as any good shop can
supply.   Indeed, I recognised it as being of
a Parisian design as yet little known in
England; while on the tops of the stockings
I laughingly suspected a border designed
by a certain eccentric artist, who devotes his
strange gifts to decorating with fascinating
miniatures the under-world of woman.   I
have seen corsets thus made beautiful by
him valued at five hundred pounds, and he
never paints a pair of garters for less than a
hundred.   His name is not yet a famous
one, as, for obvious reasons, his works are
not exhibited at public galleries, though
they are occasionally to be seen at private
views.

I am far from despising an honest red-flan-
nel country petticoat.   There is no warmer
kinder-looking garment in the world.   It
suggests country laps and country breasts,
with sturdy country babes greedy for the
warm white milk, and it seems dyed in coun-

try blushes.   Yet, for all that, one could
not be insensible to the exotic race and
distinction of that frivolous town petticoat,
daintily disporting itself there among its
country cousins, like a queen among milkmaids.

What numberless suggestions of romance
it awoke! What strange perfumes seemed to
waft across from it, perfumes laden with
associations of a world so different from the
green world where it now was, a charming
world of gay intrigue and wanton pleasure.
No wonder the wind chose it so often for its
partner as it danced through the garden,
scorning to notice the heavy homespun
things about it.   It was not every day that
that washing-day wind met so fine a lady,
and it was charming to see how gently he
played about her stockings.   "Ah, wind,"
I said, "evidently you are a gallant born;
but tell us the name of the lady.   It is somewhere on that pretty petticoat, I'll be
bound."

Is she some little danseuse with the whim
to be romantically rustic for a week? or is
she somebody else's pretty wife run away

with somebody else's man? or is she some naughty little grisette with an extravagant lover? or is she just the usual lady landscape artist, with a more than usual taste in lingerie?

At all events, it was fairly obvious that, for one reason or another, the wearer of the petticoat and stockings which have now occupied us for perhaps a sufficient number of pages, was a visitor at the cottage.

The next thing was to get a look at her. So, remembering how fond I was of milk from the cow, I pushed open the gate and advanced to the cottage door.

CHAPTER XV

STILL OCCUPIED WITH THE PETTICOAT

THE door was opened by a comely young woman, with ruddy cheeks and a bright kind eye that promised conversation. But "H'm," said I to myself, as she went to fetch my milk, "evidently not yours, my dear."

"A nice drying day for your washing," I said, as I slowly sipped my milk, with a half-inclination of my head towards the clothes-line.

"Very fine, indeed, sir," she returned, with something of a blush, and a shy depre- cating look that seemed to beg me not to notice the peculiarly quaint antics which the wind, evidently a humourist, chose at that moment to execute with the female garments upon the line. However, I was for once cased in triple brass and inexorable.

"And who," I ventured, smiling, "may be the owner of those fine things?"

"Not those," I continued, pointing to an odd garment which the wind was wantonly puffing out in the quaintest way, "but that pretty petticoat and those silk stockings?"

The poor girl had gone scarlet, scarlet as the petticoat which I was sure *was* hers, with probably a fellow at the moment keeping warm her buxom figure.

"You are very bold, sir," she stammered through her blushes, but I could see that she was not ill-pleased that the finery should attract attention.

"But won't you tell me?" I urged; "I have a reason for asking."

And here I had better warn the reader that, as the result of a whim that presently seized me, I must be content to appear mad in his eyes for the next few pages, till I get an opportunity of explanation.

"Well, what if they should be mine?" at length I persuaded her into saying.

I made the obvious gallant reply, but, "All the same," I added, "you know they are not yours. They belong to some lady visitor,

who, I 'll be bound, is n't half so pretty;
now, don't they?"

"Well, they just don't then. They 're
mine, as I tell you."

"H'm," I continued, a little nonplussed,
"but do you really mean there is no lady
staying with you?"

"Certainly," she replied, evidently enjoying my bewilderment.

"Well, then, some lady must have stayed
here once," I retorted, with a sudden inspiration, "and left them behind — "

"You might be a detective after stolen
goods," she interrupted. "I tell you the
things are mine; and what I should like to
know does a gentleman want bothering himself about a lady's petticoat! No wonder
you blush," for, in fact, as was easy to fore-
see, the situation was becoming a little
ridiculous for me.

"Now, look here," I said with an affecta-
tion of gravity, "if you 'll tell me how you
came by those things, I 'll make it worth
your while. They were given to you by a
lady who stayed here not so long ago, now,
were n't they?"

"Well, then, they were."

"The lady stayed here with a gentleman?"

"Yes, she did."

"H'm! I thought so," I said. "Yes! that lady, it pains me to say, was my wife!"

This unblushing statement was not, I could see, without its effect upon the present owner of the petticoat.

"But she said they were brother and sister," she replied.

"Of course she did," I returned, with a fine assumption of scorn, — "of course she did. They always do."

"Dear young woman," I continued, when I was able to control my emotion, "you are happily remote from the sin and wickedness of the town, and I am sorry to speak of such things in so peaceful a spot — but as a strange chance has led me here, I must speak, must tell you that all wives are not so virtuous and faithful as you, I am sure, are. There are wives who forsake their husbands and — and go off with a handsomer man, as the poet says; and mine, mine, alas! was one of them. It is now some months ago that my wife left me in this way, and since then

I have spent every day in searching for her;
but never till this moment have I come
upon the least trace of her. Strange, is it
not? that here, in this peaceful out-of-the-
way garden, I should come upon her very
petticoat, her very stockings — "

By this my grief had become such that
the kind girl put her hand on my arm.
"Don't take on so," she said kindly, and
then remembering her treasured property,
and probably fearing a counterclaim on my
part to its possession, "But how can you
be sure she was here? There are lots of
petticoats like that — "

"What was she like?" I asked through
my agitation.

"Middle height, slim and fair, with red
goldy hair and big blue eyes; about thirty, I
should say."

"The very same," I groaned, "there is
no mistake; and now," I continued, "I want
you to sell me that petticoat and those
stockings," and I took a couple of sovereigns
from my purse. "I want to have them to
confront her with, when I do find her. Perhaps it will touch her heart to think of the

strange way in which I came by them; and you can buy just as pretty ones again with the money," I added, as I noticed the disappointment on her face at the prospect of thus losing her finery.

" Well, it's a funny business, to be sure," she said, as still half reluctantly she unpegged the coveted garments from the line; " but if what you say's true, I suppose you must have them."

The wanton wind had been so busily kissing them all the morning that they were quite dry, so I was able to find room for them in my knapsack without danger to the other contents; and, with a hasty good-day to their recent possessor, I set off at full speed to find a secure nook where I could throw myself down on the grass, and let loose the absurd laughter that was dangerously bottled up within me; but even before I do that it behoves me if possible to vindicate my sanity to the reader.

CHAPTER XVI

CLEARS UP MY MYSTERIOUS BEHAVIOUR OF THE LAST CHAPTER

WHAT a sane man should be doing carrying about with him a woman's petticoat and silk stockings, may well be a puzzle to the most intelligent reader.

Whim, sir, whim! and few human actions admit of more satisfactory solution. Like Shylock, I'll say "It is my humour." But no! I'll be more explanatory. This madcap quest of mine, was it not understood between us from the beginning to be a fantastic whim, a poetical wild-goose chase, conceived entirely as an excuse for being some time in each other's company? To be whimsical, therefore, in pursuit of a whim, fanciful in the chase of a fancy, is surely but to maintain the spirit of the game. Now, for the purpose, therefore, of a romance that makes no pretence to reasonableness, I had very good reasons for buying that petticoat, which (the reasons, not the petticoat) I will now lay before you.

I have been conscious all the way along through this pilgrimage of its inevitable vagueness of direction, of my need of something definite, some place, some name, anything at all, however slight, which I might associate, if only for a time, with the object of my quest, a definite something to seek, a definite goal for my feet.

Now, when I saw that mysterious petticoat, and realised that its wearer would probably be pretty and young and generally charming, and that probably her name was somewhere on the waistband, the spirit of whim rejoiced within me. " Why not," it said, " buy the petticoat, find out the name of its owner, and, instead of seeking a vague Golden Girl, make up your mind doggedly to find and marry her, or, failing that, carry the petticoat with you, as a sort of Cinderella's slipper, try it on any girl you happen to fancy, and marry her it exactly fits? "

Now, I confess, that seemed to me quite

a pretty idea, and I hope the reader will think so too. If not, I'm afraid I can offer him no better explanation; and in fact I am all impatience to open my knapsack, and inform myself of the name of her to the discovery of whom my wanderings are henceforth to be devoted.

6

CHAPTER XVII

THE NAME UPON THE PETTICOAT

So imagine me seated in a grassy corner,
with my knapsack open on the ground and
my petticoat and silk stockings spread out
in front of me, — an odd picture, to be sure,
for any passer by to come upon. I suppose
I could have passed for a pedlar, but
undoubtedly it would have been very embarrassing. However, as it happened, I remained
undisturbed, and was able to examine my
purchases at leisure. I had never seen a
petticoat so near before, — at all events I had
never given one such close attention. What
delicious dainty things they are! How essentially womanly — as I hope no one would
call a pair of trousers essentially manly.

How pretty it looked spread out on the
grass in front of me! How soft! how won-

drously dainty the finish of every little seam!
And the lace! It almost tempts one to
change one's sex to wear such things. There
was a time indeed, and not so long ago,
when brave men wore garments no less
dainty. Rupert's Cavaliers were every bit
as particular about their lace collars and frills
as the lady whose pretty limbs once warmed
this cambric.

But where is the name? Ah! here it is!
What sweet writing! "*Sylvia Joy, No. 6.*"

Sylvia Joy! What a perfectly enchanting
name! and as I repeated it enthusiastically,
it seemed to have a certain familiarity for
my ear, — as though it were the name of
some famous beauty or some popular actress,
— yet the exact association eluded me, and
obviously it was better it should remain a
name of mystery. Sylvia Joy! Who could
have hoped for such a pretty name! Indeed,
to tell the truth, I had dreaded to find a
"Mary Jones" or an "Ann Williams" —
but Sylvia Joy! The name was a romance
in itself. I already felt myself falling in
love with its unseen owner. With such a
petticoat and such a name, Sylvia herself

could not be otherwise than delightful too. Already, you see, I was calling her by her Christian name! And the more I thought of her, the stronger grew the conviction — which has no doubt already forced itself upon the romantic reader — that we were born for each other.

But who is Sylvia, who is she? and likewise where is Sylvia, where is she? Obviously they were questions not to be answered off-hand. Was not my future — at all events my immediate future — to be spent in answering them?

Indeed, curiously enough, my recent haste to have them answered had suddenly died down. A sort of matrimonial security possessed me. I felt as I imagine a husband may feel on a solitary holiday — if there are husbands unnatural enough to go holidaying without their wives — pleasantly conscious of a home tucked somewhere beneath the distant sunset, yet in no precipitate hurry to return there before the appointed day.

In fact, a chill tremor went through me as I realised that, to all intent, I was at length respectably settled down, with quite a con-

siderable retrospect of happy married life.
To come to a decision is always to bring
something to an end.   And, with something
of a pang, resolutely stifled, I realised for a
moment the true blessedness of the single
state I was so soon to leave behind.   At all
events, a little golden fragment of bachelor-
hood remained.   There was yet a fertile
strip of time wherein to sow my last handful
of the wild oats of youth.   So *festina lente*,
my destined Sylvia, *festina lente !*

CHAPTER XVIII

IN WHICH THE NAME OF A GREAT POET IS CRIED OUT IN A SOLITARY PLACE

As I once more shouldered my pack and went my way, the character of the country-side began to change, and, from a semi-pastoral heathiness and furziness, took on a wildness of aspect, which if indeed melo-dramatic was melodrama carried to the point of genius. It was a scene for which the nineteenth century has no worthy use. It finds ignoble occupation as a gaping-ground for the vacuous tourist, — somewhat as Heine might have imagined Pan carrying the gentle-man's luggage from the coach to the hotel. It suffers teetotal picnic-parties to encamp amid its savage hollows, and it humbly allows itself to be painted by the worst artists. Like a lion in a menagerie, it is a survival of the extinct chaos entrapped and exhibited

amid the smug parks and well-rolled downs
of England.

I came upon it by a winding ledge of road,
which clung to the bare side of the hill like
the battlements of some huge castle. Some
two hundred feet below, a brawling upland
stream stood for the moat, and for the enemy
there was on the opposite side of the valley a
great green company of trees, settled like a
cloud slope upon slope, making all haste to
cross the river and ascend the heights where
I stood. Some intrepid larches waved green
pennons in the very midst of the turbulent
water, here and there a veteran lay with his
many-summered head abased in the rocky
course of the stream, and here was a young
foolhardy beech that had climbed within a
dozen yards of the rampart. All was wild
and solitary, and one might have declared it
a scene untrodden by the foot of man, but
for the telegraph posts and small piles of
broken "macadam" at punctual intervals,
and the ginger-beer bottles and paper bags
of local confectioners that lent an air of
civilisation to the road.

It was a place to quote *Alastor* in, and

nothing but a bad memory prevented my
affrighting the oaks and rills with declama-
tion. As it was, I could only recall the lines

> "The Poet wandering on, through Arabie
> And Persia, and the wild Carmanian waste,
> And o'er the aerial mountains which pour down
> Indus and Oxus from their icy caves —"

and that other passage beginning

> "At length upon the lone Chorasmian shore
> He paused —"

This last I mouthed, loving the taste of its
thunder; mouthed thrice, as though it were an
incantation, — and, indeed, from what immediately followed, it might reasonably have
seemed so.

> "At length upon the lone Chorasmian shore
> He paused —"

I mouthed for the fourth time. And lo!
advancing to me eagerly along the causeway
seemed the very sprite of Alastor himself!
There was a star upon his forehead, and
around his young face there glowed an
aureole of gold and roses — to speak figura-
tively, for the star upon his brow was hope,

and the gold and roses encircling his head, a miniature rainbow, were youth and health. His longish golden hair had no doubt its share in the effect, as likewise the soft yellow silk tie that fluttered like a flame in the speed of his going. His blue eyes were tragically fresh and clear, — as though they had as yet been little used. There were little wings of haste upon his feet, and he came straight to me, with the air of the Angel Gabriel about to make his divine announcement. For a moment I thought that he was an apparition of prophecy charged to announce the maiden of the Lord for whom I was seeking. However, his brief flushed question was not of these things. He desired first to ask the time of day, and next — here, after a bump to the earth, one's thoughts ballooned again heavenwards — " had I seen a green copy of Shelley lying anywhere along the road?"

Nothing so good had happened to me, I replied — but I believed that I had seen a copy of Alastor! For a moment my meaning was lost on him; then he flushed and smiled, thanked me and was off again, say-

ing that he must find his Shelley, as he
would n't lose it for the world!

He had presently disappeared as suddenly
as he had come, but he had left me a companion, a radiant reverberant name; and for
some little space the name of Shelley clashed
silvery music among the hills.

Its seven letters seemed to hang right
across the clouds like the Seven Stars, an
apocalyptic constellation, a veritable sky-
sign; and again the name was an angel standing with a silver trumpet, and again it was a
song. The heavens opened, and across the
blue rift it hung in a glory of celestial fire,
while from behind and above the clouds
came a warbling as of innumerable larks.

How strange was this miracle of fame,
I pondered, this strange apotheosis by
which a mere private name becomes a public
symbol! Shelley was once a private person
whose name had no more universal meaning
than my own, and so were Byron and Crom-
well and Shakespeare; yet now their names
are facts as stubborn as the Rocky Mountains,
or the National Gallery, or the circulation of
the blood. From their original inch or so

of private handwriting they have spread and spread out across the world, and now whole generations of men find intellectual accommodation within them, — drinking fountains and other public institutions are erected upon them; yea, Carlyle has become a Chelsea swimming-bath, and "Highland Mary" is sold for whiskey, while Mr. Gladstone is to be met everywhere in the form of a bag.

Does Mr. Gladstone, I wonder, instruct his valet "to pack his Gladstone"? How strange it must seem! Try it yourself some day and its effect on your servant. Ask him, for example, to "pack your —— " and see how he'll stare.

Coming nearer and nearer to earth, I wondered if Colonel Boycott ever uses the word "boycott," and how strange it must have seemed to the late MacAdam to walk for miles and miles upon his own name, like a carpet spread out before him.

Then I once more rebounded heavenwards, at the vision of the eager dreamy lad whose question had set going all this odd clockwork of association. He would n't lose his Shelley for the world! How like twenty!

And how many things that he would n't lose
for the world will he have to give up before
he is thirty, I reflected sententiously, — give
up at last, maybe, with a stony indifference,
as men on a sinking ship take no thought of
the gold and specie in the hold.

And then, all of a sudden, a little way up
the ferny grassy hillside, I caught sight of
the end of a book half hidden among the
ferns. I climbed up to it. Of course it was
that very green Shelley which the young
stranger would n't lose for the world.

CHAPTER XIX

WHY THE STRANGER WOULD NOT LOSE HIS SHELLEY FOR THE WORLD

PICKING up the book, I opened it involuntarily at the titlepage, and then — I resisted a great temptation! I shut it again. A little flowery plot of girl's handwriting had caught my eye, and a girl's pretty name. When Love and Beauty meet, it is hard not to play the eavesdropper, and it was easy to guess that Love and Beauty met upon that page. St. Anthony had no harder fight with the ladies he was unpolite enough to call demons, than I in resisting the temptation to take another look at that pen-and-ink lovemaking. Now, as I look back, I think it was sheer priggishness to resist so human and yet so reverent an impulse. There is nothing sacred from reverence, and love's lovers have a right to regard themselves as the confidants of lovers, whenever they may chance to surprise either them or their letters.

While I was still hesitating, and wondering how I could get the book conveyed to its romantic owner, suddenly a figure turned the corner of the road, and there was Alastor coming back again. I slipped the book, in distracted search for which he was evidently still engaged, under the ferns, and, leisurely lighting a pipe, prepared to tease him. He was presently within hail, and, looking up, caught sight of me.

" Have you found your Shelley yet ? " I called down to him, as he stood a moment in the road.

He shook his head. No! But he meant to find it, if he had to hunt every square foot of the valley inch by inch.

Would n't any other book do, I asked him. Would he take a Boccaccio, or a " Golden Ass," or a " Tom Jones," in exchange? — for of such consisted my knapsack library. He laughed a negative, and it seemed a shame to tease him.

" It is not so much the book itself," he said.

" But the giver? " I suggested.

" Of course," he blushingly replied.

" Well, suppose I have found it? " I continued.

" You don't mean it — "

" But suppose I have — I 'm only supposing — will you give me the pleasure of your company at dinner at the next inn and tell me its story? "

" Indeed I will, gladly," he replied.

" Well, then," I said, " catch, for here it is ! "

The joy with which he recovered it was pretty to behold, and the eagerness with which he ran through the leaves, to see that the violets and the primroses and a spray of meadowsweet, young love's bookmarkers, were all in their right places, touched my heart.

He could not thank me enough; and as we stepped out to the inn, some three or four miles on the road, I elicited something of his story.

He was a clerk in a city office, he said, but his dreams were not commercial. His one dream was to be a great poet, or a great writer of some sort, and this was one of his

holidays.   As I looked at his sensitive young
face, unmarred by pleasure and unscathed
by sorrow, bathed daily, I surmised, in the
may-dew of high philosophies — ah, so high!
washed from within by a constant radiancy
of pure thoughts, and from without by a
constant basking in the shine of every
beautiful and noble and tender thing, — I
thought it not unlikely that he might fulfil
his dream.

But, alas! as he talked on, with lighted
face and chin in the air, how cruelly I
realised how little I had fulfilled mine.

And how hard it was to talk to him, without crushing some flower of his fancy or
casting doubt upon his dreams. Oh, the
gulf between twenty and thirty! I had
never quite comprehended it before. And
how inexpressibly sad it was to hear him
prattling on of the ideal life, of socialism,
of Walt Whitman and what not, — all the
dear old quackeries, — while I was already
settling down comfortably to a conservative
middle age. He had no hope that had not
long been my despair, no aversion that I had
not accepted among the more or less com-

fortable conditions of the universe.   He was all for nature and liberty, whereas I had now come to realise the charm of the arti- ficial, and the social value of constraint.

"Young man," I cried in my heart, "what shall I do to inherit Eternal Youth?"

The gulf between us was further revealed when, at length coming to our inn, we sat down to dinner.   To me it seemed the most natural thing in the world to call for the wine-list and consult his choice of wine; but, will you believe me, he asked to be allowed to drink water!   And when he quoted the dear old stock nonsense out of Thoreau about being able to get intoxicated on a glass of water, I could have laughed and cried at the same time.

"Happy Boy!" I cried, "still able to turn water into wine by the divine power of your youth"; and then, turning to the waiter, I ordered a bottle of No. 37.

"Wine is the only youth granted to middle age," I continued, — "*in vino juventus*, one might say; and may you, my dear young friend, long remain so proudly independent of that great Elixir — though I confess that

7

I have met no few young men under thirty who have been excellent critics of the wine-list."

As the water warmed him, he began to expand into further confidence, and then he told me the story of his Shelley, if a story it can be called. For, of course, it was simple enough, and the reader has long since guessed that the reason why he would n't lose his Shelley for the world was the usual simple reason.

I listened to his rhapsodies of *Her* and *Her* and *Her* with an aching heart. How good it was to be young! No wonder men had so desperately sought the secret of Eternal Youth! Who would not be young for ever, for such dreams and such an appetite?

Here of course was the very heaven-sent confidant for such an enterprise as mine. I told him all about my whim, just for the pleasure of watching his face light up with youth's generous worship of all such fantastic nonsense. You should have seen his enthusiasm and heard all the things he said. Why, to encounter such a whimsical fellow

as myself in this unimaginative age was like
meeting a fairy prince, or coming unexpectedly upon Don Quixote attacking the
windmill.   I offered him the post of Sancho
Panza; and indeed what would he not give,
he said, to leave all and follow me!   But
then I reminded him that he had already
found his Golden Girl.

"Of course, I forgot," he said, with I'm
afraid something of a sigh.   For you see
he was barely twenty, and to have met
your ideal so early in life is apt to rob
the remainder of the journey of something
of its zest.

I asked him to give me his idea of what
the Blessed Maid should be, to which he
replied, with a smile, that he could not do
better than describe Her, which he did for
the sixth time.   It was, as I had foreseen,
the picture of a Saint, a Goddess, a Dream,
very lovely and pure and touching; but it
was not a woman, and it was a woman I was
in search of, with all her imperfections on
her head.   I suppose no boy of twenty
really loves a *woman*, but loves only his
etherealised extract of woman, entirely free

from earthy adulteration.   I noticed the
words "pure" and "natural" in constant use
by my young friend.   Some lines went
through my head, but I forbore to quote
them : —

> Alas! your so called purity
> Is merely immaturity,
> And woman's nature plays its part
> Sincerely but in woman's art.

But I could n't resist asking him, out of
sheer waggery, whether he did n't think a
touch of powder, and even, very judiciously
applied, a touch of rouge, was an improve-
ment to woman.   His answer went to my
heart.

"Paint — *a woman!*" he exclaimed.

It was as though you had said — paint an
angel!

I could bear no more of it.   The gulf
yawned shiveringly wide at remarks like
that; so, with the privilege of an elder, I
declared it time for bed, and yawned off to
my room.

Next morning we bade good-bye, and went
our several ways.   As we parted, he handed
me a letter which I was not to open till I

was well on my journey. We waved good-bye
to each other till the turnings of the road
made parting final, and then, sitting down
by the roadside, I opened the letter. It
proved to be not a letter, but a poem, which
he had evidently written after I had left
him for bed. It was entitled, with twenty's
love for a tag of Latin, *Ad Puellam Auream*,
and it ran thus : —

> The Golden Girl in every place
> Hides and reveals her lovely face ;
> Her neither skill nor strength may find —
> 'T is only loving moves her mind.
> If but a pretty face you seek,
> You 'll find one any day or week ;
> But if you look with deeper eyes,
> And seek her lovely, pure, and wise,
> Then must you wear the pilgrim's shoon
> For many a weary, wandering moon.
>
> Only the pure in heart may see
> That lily of all purity,
> Only in clean unsullied thought
> The image of her face is caught,
> And only he her love may hold
> Who buys her with the spirit's gold.
>
> Thus only shall you find your pearl,
> O seeker of the Golden Girl !
> She trod but now the grassy way,
> A vision of eternal May.

The devil take his impudence! "Only the pure in heart," "clean, unsullied thought." How like the cheek of twenty! And all the same how true! Dear lad, how true! Certainly, the child is father to the man. *Dirige nos!* O sage of the Golden Twenties!

As I meditatively folded up the pretty bit of writing, I made a resolution; but it was one of such importance that not only is another chapter needed to do it honour, but it may well inaugurate another book of this strange uneventful history.

BOOK II

CHAPTER I

IN WHICH I DECIDE TO BE YOUNG AGAIN

YES, I said to myself, the lad is quite right; I will follow his advice. I'm afraid I was in danger of developing into a sad cynic, with a taste for the humour of this world. What should have been a lofty high-souled pilgrimage, only less transcendental than that of the Holy Grail itself, has so far failed, no doubt, because I have undertaken it too much in the wanton spirit of a troubadour.

I will grow young and serious again. Yes, why not? I will take a vow of Youth. One's age is entirely a matter of the imagination. From this moment I am no longer thirty. Thirty falls from me like a hideous dream. My back straightens again at the thought; my silvering hair blackens once more; my eyes, a few moments ago lacklustre and sunken, grow bright and full again, and the whites are clear as the finest porcelain. *Veni, veni, Mephistophile!* your Faust is young again, — young, young, and, with a boy's heart, open once more to all the influences of the mighty world.

I bring down my stick upon the ground with a mighty ring of resolution, and the miracle is done. Who would take me for thirty now? From this moment I abjure pessimism and cynicism in all their forms, put from my mind all considerations of the complexities of human life, unravel all by a triumphant optimism which no statistics can abash or criticism dishearten. I likewise undertake to divest myself entirely of any sense of humour that may have developed within me during the baneful experiences of the last ten years, and, in short, will consent for the future to be nothing that is not perfectly perfect and pure. These, I take it, are the fundamental conditions of being young again.

And as for the Quest, it shall forthwith

be undertaken in an entirely serious and high-minded spirit. From this moment I am on the look-out for a really transcendental attachment. No "bright-eyed bar-maids," however "refined," need apply. Ladies who are prodigal of their white petticoats are no longer fit company for me. Indeed I shall no longer look upon a petticoat, unless I am able first entirely to spiritualise it. It must first be disinfected of every earthly thought.

Yes, I am once more a young man, sound in wind and limb, with not a tooth or an illusion lost, my mind *tabula rasa*, my heart to be had for the asking. Oh, come, ye merry, merry maidens! The fairy prince is on the fairy road.

Incipit vita nuova !

So in the lovely rapture of a new-born resolution — and is there any rapture like it? — nature has no more intoxicating illusion than that of turning over a new leaf, or beginning a new life from to-day — I sprang along the road with a carolling heart ; quite forgetting that Apuleius and Fielding and Boccaccio were still in my knapsack — not to speak of the petticoat.

CHAPTER II

AT THE SIGN OF THE SINGING STREAM

APULEIUS and Fielding and Boccaccio, bad companions for a petticoat, I'm afraid, bad companions too for so young a man as I had now become. However, as I say, I had for the time forgotten that pagan company, or, in my puritanic zeal, I might have thrown them all to be washed clean in the upland stream, whose pure waters one might fancy were fragrant from their sunny day among the ferns and the heather, fragrant to the eye, indeed, if one may so speak, with the shaken meal of the meadowsweet. This stream had been the good angel of my thoughts all the day, keeping them ever moving and ever fresh, cleansing and burnishing them, quite an open-air laundry of the mind.

We were both making for the same little town, it appeared, and as the sun was setting we reached it together. I entered the

town over the bridge, and the stream under
it, washing the walls of the high-piled,
many-gabled old inn where I proposed to
pass the night.   I should hear it still rippling on with its gentle harpsichord tinkle,
as I stretched myself down among the cool
lavendered sheets, and little by little let slip
the multifarious world.

The inn windows beamed cheerily, a home
of ruddy rest.   Having ordered my dinner
and found my room, I threw down my knapsack and then came out again to smoke an
ante-prandial pipe, listen to the evensong of
the stream, and think great thoughts.   The
stream was still there, and singing the same
sweet old song.   You could hear it long
after it was out of sight, in the gathering
darkness, like an old nurse humming lulla-
bies in the twilight.

The dinner was good, the wine was old,
and oh! the rest was sweet!   Nothing fills
one with so exquisite a weariness as a day
spent in good resolutions and great thoughts.
There is something perilously sensuous in
the relaxation of one's muscles, both of mind
and body, after a day thus well spent.

Lighting up my pipe once more, and drawing to the fire, I suddenly realised a sense
of loneliness.   Of course, I was lonely for a
book, — Apuleius or Fielding or Boccaccio!

An hour ago they had seemed dangerous
companions for so lofty a mood; but now,
under the gentle influences of dinner, the
mood had not indeed changed — but mellowed.   So to say, we would split the dif-
ference between the ideal and the human,
and be, say, twenty-five.

It was in this genial attitude of mind that
I strode up the quaint circular staircase to
fetch Fielding from my room, and, shade of
Tom Jones! what should be leaving my
room, as I advanced to enter it, but — well,
it's no use, resolutions are all very well,
but facts are facts, especially when they're
natural, and here was I face to face with the
most natural little natural fact, and withal
the most charming and merry-eyed, that —
well, in short, as I came to enter my room
I was confronted by the roundest, ruddiest
little chambermaid ever created for the trial
of mortal frailty.

And the worst of it was that her merry eye

was in partnership with a merry tongue.
Indeed, for some unexplained reason, she
was bubbling over with congested laughter,
the reason for which mere embarrassment
set one inquiring.   At last, between little
gushes of laughter which shook her plump
shoulders in a way that aroused wistful
memories of Hebe, she archly asked me,
with mock solemnity, if I should need a
lady's maid.

"Certainly," I replied with inane prompti-
tude, for I had no notion of her drift; but
then she ran off in a scurry of laughter, and
still puzzled I turned into my room, *to find*,
neatly hung over the end of the bed, nothing
less than the dainty petticoat and silk stockings of Sylvia Joy.

You can imagine the colour of my cheeks
at the discovery.   No doubt I was already
the laughing-stock of the whole inn.   What
folly!   What a young vixen!   Oh, what's
to be done?   Pay my bill and sneak off at
once to the next town; but how pass through
the grinning line of boots, and waiter, and
chambermaid, and ironically respectful landlord and landlady, in the hall . . .

But while I thus deliberated, something soft pressed in at the door; and, making a sudden dart, I had the little baggage who had brought about my dilemma a prisoner in my arms.

I stayed some days at this charming old inn, for Amaryllis — oh, yes, you may be sure her name was Amaryllis — had not betrayed me; and indeed she may have some share in my retrospect of the inn as one of the most delightful which I encountered anywhere in my journeying. Would you like to know its name? Well, I know it as The Singing Stream. If you can find it under that name, you are welcome. And should you chance to be put into bedroom No. 26, you can think of me, and how I used to lie awake, listening to the stream rippling beneath the window, with its gentle harpsichord tinkle, and little by little letting slip the multifarious world.

And if anything about this chapter should seem to contradict the high ideals of the chapter preceding it, I can only say that, though the episode should not rigidly fulfil the conditions of the transcendental, nothing could have been more characteristic of that early youth to which I had vowed myself.   Indeed, I congratulated myself, as I looked my last at the sign of The Singing Stream, that this had been quite in my early manner.

CHAPTER III

IN WHICH I SAVE A USEFUL LIFE

THOUGH I had said good-bye to the inn, the stream and I did not part company at the inn-door, but continued for the best part of a morning to be fellow-travellers. Indeed, having led me to one pleasant adventure, its purpose, I afterwards realised, was to lead me to another, and then to go about its own bright business. I don't think either of us had much idea where we were or whither we were bound. Our guiding principle seemed to be to get as much sunshine as possible, and to find the easiest road. We avoided dull sandy levels and hard rocky places, with the same instinctive dexterity. We gloomed together through dark dingles, and came out on sunny reaches with the same gilded magnificence. There are days when every stream is Pactolus and every man is Crœsus, and

thanks to that first and greatest of all alche-
mists, the sun, the morning I write of was
a morning when to breathe was gold and to
see was silver.   And to breathe and see was
all one asked.   It was the first of May, and
the world shone like a great illuminated
letter with which that father of artists, the
sun, was making splendid his missal of the
seasons.

The month of May was ever his *tour de
force.*   Each year he has strained and stimu-
lated his art to surpass himself, seeking ever
a finer and a brighter gold, a more celestial
azure.   Never had his gold been so golden,
his azure so dazzlingly clear and deep as
on this particular May morning; while his
fancy simply ran riot in the marginal dec-
orations of woodland and spinney, quaint
embroidered flowers and copses full of exquisitely painted and wonderfully trained
birds of song.   It was indeed a day for nature to be proud of.   So seductive was the
sunshine that even the shy trout leapt at
noonday, eager apparently to change his silver for gold.

O silver fish in the silver stream,
O golden fish in the golden gleam,
Tell me, tell me, tell me true,
Shall I find my girl if I follow you?

I suppose the reader never makes non-sense rhymes from sheer gladness of heart, — nursery doggerel to keep time with the rippling of the stream, or the dancing of the sun, or the beating of his heart; the gibberish of delight. As I hummed this nonsense, a trout at least three pounds in weight, whom you would know again anywhere, leapt a yard out of the water, and I took it, in my absurd, sun-soaked heart, as a good omen, as though he had said, "Follow and see."

I had no will but to follow, no desire but to see. All the same, though I affected to take him seriously, I had little suspicion how much that trout was to mean to me, — yes, within the course of a very few moments. Indeed, I had hardly strolled on for another quarter of a mile, when I was suddenly aroused from wool-gathering by his loud cries for help. Looking up, I saw him flashing desperately in mid-air, a lovely foot

of writhing silver. In another second he
was swung through the sunlight, and laid
out breathing hard in a death-bed of butter-
cups and daisies. There was not a moment
to be lost, if I were to repay the debt of
gratitude which in a flash I had seen that I
owed him.

"Madam," I said, breathlessly springing
forward, as a heavenly being was coldly
tearing the hook from the gills of the
unlucky trout, "though I am a stranger,
will you do me a great favour? It is a
matter of life or death . . ."

She looked up at me with some surprise,
but with a fine fearless glance, and almost immediately said, "Certainly, what can I do?"

"Spare the life of that trout — "

"It is a singular request," she replied,
"and one," she smiled, "self-sacrificing indeed for an angler to grant, for he weighs
at least three pounds. However, since he
seems a friend of yours, here goes — " And
with the gladdest, most grateful sound in
the world, the happy smack of a fish back
home again in the water, after an appalling
three minutes spent on land, that prophetic

trout was once more an active unit in God's populous universe.

"Now that's good of you," I said, with thankful eyes, "and shows a kind heart."

"And kind hearts, they say, are more than coronets," she replied merrily, indulging in that derisive quotation which seems to be the final reward of the greatest poets.

For a moment there was a silence, during which I confess to wondering what I should say next. However, she supplied my place.

"But of course," she said, "you owe it to me, after this touching display of humanitarianism, to entertain me with your reason for interposing between me and my just trout. Was it one of those wonderful talking fishes out of the Arabian Nights, or are you merely an angler yourself, and did you begrudge such a record catch to a girl?"

"I see," I replied, "that you will understand me. That trout *was*, so to speak, out of the Arabian Nights. Only five minutes ago it was a May-day madness of mine to think that he leaped out of the water and gave me a highly important message. So I begged his life from a mere fancy. It was just a whim, which I trust you will excuse."

"A whim! So you are a follower of the great god Whim," she replied, with somewhat of an eager interest in her voice. "How nice it is to meet a fellow-worshipper!"

"Do women ever have whims?" I respectfully asked.

"I don't know about other women," she replied. "Indeed, I'm afraid I'm unnatural enough to take no interest in them at all. But, as for me, — well, what nonsense! Tell me some more about the trout. What was the wonderful message he seemed to give you? Or perhaps I ought n't to ask?"

"I'm afraid," I said, "it would hardly translate into anything approaching common-sense."

"Did I ask for common-sense?" she retorted. It was true, she had n't. But then I could n't, with any respect for her, tell her the trout's message, or, with any respect for myself, recall those atrocious doggerel lines. In my dilemma, I caught sight of a pretty book lying near her fishing-basket, and diverted the talk by venturing to ask its name.

"'T is of Aucassin and Nicolete," she replied, with something in her voice which seemed to imply that the tender old story would be familiar to me. My memory served me for once gallantly. I answered by humming half to myself the lines from the prologue, —

> " Sweet the song, the story sweet,
>   There is no man hearkens it,
>   No man living 'neath the sun,
>   So outwearied, so foredone,
>   Sick and woful, worn and sad,
>   But is healèd, but is glad
>   'T is so sweet."

"How charming of you to know it!" she laughed. "You are the only man in this county, or the next, or the next, who knows it, I 'm sure."

"Are the women of the county more familiar with it?" I replied.

"But tell me about the trout," she once more persisted.

At the same moment, however, there came from a little distance the musical tinkle of a bell that sounded like silver, a fairy-like and almost startling sound.

"It is my lunch," she explained. "I'm a worshipper of the great god Whim too, and close by here I have a little summer-house, full of books and fishing-lines and other childishness, where, when my whim is to be lonely, I come and play at solitude. If you'll be content with rustic fare, and promise to be amusing, it would be very pleasant if you'd join me."

O! most prophetic and agreeable trout! Was it not like the old fairy tales, the you-help-us and we'll-help-you of Psyche and the ants?

It had been the idlest whim for me to save the life of that poor trout. There was no real pity in it. For two pins, I had been just as ready to cut it open, to see if by chance it carried in its belly the golden ring wherewith I was to wed the Golden —

However, such is the gratitude of nature to man, that this little thoughtless act of kindness had brought me face to face with — was it the Golden Girl?

CHAPTER IV

'T IS OF NICOLETE AND HER BOWER IN THE WILDWOOD

BUT I have all this time left the reader without any formal descriptive introduction to this whimsical young lady angler. Not without reason, for, like any really charming personality, she was very difficult to picture. Paint a woman! as our young friend Alastor said.

Faces that fall into types you can describe, or at all events label in such a way that the reader can identify them; but those faces that consist mainly of spiritual effect and physical bloom, that change with everything they look upon, the light in which ebbs and flows with every changing tide of the soul, — these you have to love to know, and to worship to portray.

Now the face of Nicolete, as I learnt in time to call her, was just soul and bloom, perhaps mainly bloom. I never noticed whether she had any other features except her eyes. I suppose she had a nose; a little lace pocket-handkerchief I have by me at the moment is almost too small to be evidence on that important point.

As I walked by her side that May morning, I was only conscious of her voice and her exquisite girlhood; for though she talked with the *aplomb* of a woman of the world, a passionate candour and simple ardour in her manner would have betrayed her, had her face not plainly declared her the incarnation of twenty. But if she were twenty years young, she was equally twenty years *old ;* and twenty years old, in some respects, is the greatest age attained to by man or woman. In this she rather differed from Alastor, of whom otherwise she was the female counterpart. Her talk, and something rather in her voice than her talk, soon revealed her as a curious mixture of youth and age, of dreamer and *désillusionée.* One soon realised that she was too young, was hoping too much from life, to spend one's days with. Yet she had just sufficiently

that touch of languor which puts one at
one's ease, though indeed it was rather the
languor of waiting for what was going to
happen than the weariness of experience
gone by. She was weary, not because of the
past, but because the fairy theatre of life
still kept its curtain down, and forced her to
play over and over again the impatient over-
ture of her dreams.

I have no doubt that it was largely nervousness that kept the mysterious playwright
so long fumbling behind the scenes, for it
was obvious that it would be no ordinary
sort of play, no every-day domestic drama,
that would satisfy this young lady, to whom
life had given, by way of prologue, the in-
estimable blessing of wealth, and the privilege, as a matter of course, of choosing as she
would among the grooms (that is, the bride-
grooms) of the romantic British aristocracy.

She had made youth's common mistake of
beginning life with books, which can only
be used without danger by those who are in
a position to test their statements. Youth
naturally believes everything that is told it,
especially in books.

Now, books are simply professional liars
about life, and the books that are best worth
reading are those which lie the most beautifully.   Yet, in fairness, we must add that
they are liars, not with intent to mislead,
but merely with the tenderest purpose to
console.   They are the good Samaritans
that find us robbed of all our dreams by the
roadside of life, bleeding and weeping and
desolate; and such is their skill and wealth
and goodness of heart, that they not only
heal up our wounds, but restore to us the
lost property of our dreams, on one condition, — that we never travel with them
again in the daylight.

A library is a better world, built by the
brains and hearts of poets and dreamers, as
a refuge from the real world outside; and in
it alone is to be found the land of milk and
honey which it promises.

"Milk and honey" would have been an
appropriate inscription for the delicious
little library which parents who, I surmised,
doted on Nicolete in vain, had allowed her
to build in a wild woodland corner of her
ancestral park, half a mile away from the

great house, where, for all its corridors and
galleries, she could never feel, at all events,
spiritually alone.   All that was most sugared
and musical and generally delusive in the
old library of her fathers had been brought
out to this little woodland library, and to
that nucleus of old leather-bound poets and
romancers, long since dead, yet as alive and
singing on their shelves as any bird on the
sunny boughs outside, my young lady's
private purse had added all that was most
sugared and musical and generally delusive
in the vellum-bound Japanese-paper literature of our own luxurious day.   Nor were
poets and romancers from over sea — in their
seeming simple paper covers, but with, oh,
such complicated and subtle insides! — absent from the court which Nicolete held here
in the greenwood.   Never was such a nest of
singing-birds.   All day long, to the ear of
the spirit, there was in this little library a
sound of harping and singing and the telling
of tales, — songs and tales of a world that
never was, yet shall ever be.   Here day by
day Nicolete fed her young soul on the
nightingale's-tongues of literature, and put

down her book only to listen to the nightingale's-tongues outside.   Yea, sun, moon,
and stars were all in the conspiracy to lie to
her of the loveliness of the world and the
good intentions of life.   And now, thus
unexpectedly, I found myself joining the
nefarious conspiracy.   Ah, well ! was I not
twenty myself, and full of dreams!

CHAPTER V

'T IS OF AUCASSIN AND NICOLETE

THUS it was that we lunched together amid the books and birds, in an exquisite solitude *à deux;* for the ringer of the silver bell had disappeared, having left a dainty meal in readiness — for two.

"You see you were expected," said Nicolete, with her pretty laugh. "I dreamed I should have a visitor to-day, and told Susan to lay the lunch for two. You must n't be surprised at that," she added mischievously; "it has often happened before. I dream that dream every other night, and Susan lays for two every day. She knows my whims, — knows that the extra knife and fork are for the fairy knight that may turn up any afternoon, as I tell her —"

"To find the sleepless princess," I added, thinking at the same time one of those irrel-

evant asides that will go through the brain
of thirty, that the woman who would get
her share of kisses nowadays must neither
slumber nor sleep.

A certain great poet, I think it was Byron,
objected to seeing women in the act of eating. He thought their eating should be
done in private. What a curiously perverse
opinion! For surely woman never shows to
better advantage than in the dainty exercises
of a dainty repast, and there is nothing more
thrilling to man than a meal alone with a
woman he loves or is about to love. Perhaps, deep down, the reason is that there
still vibrates in the masculine blood the
thrilling surprise of the moment when man
first realised that the angel woman was built
upon the same carnivorous principles as his
grosser self.

That is one of the first heart-beating sur-
prises that come upon the boy Columbus, as
he sets out to discover the New World of
woman; and indeed his surprise has not
seldom deepened into admiration, as he has
found that not only does woman eat, but
frequently eats a lot.

This privilege of seeing woman eat is the earliest granted of those delicate animal intimacies, the fuller and fuller confiding of which plays not the least important part, and ever such a sweet one, even in a highly transcendental affection. It is this gradual humanising of the divine female that brings about the spiritualising of the unregenerate male.

In the earliest stages of love the services are small that we are privileged to do for the loved one. But if we are allowed to sit at meat with her, — ever a royal condescension, — it is ours at least to pass her the salt, to see that she is never kept waiting a moment for the mustard or the pepper, to cut the bread for her with geometrical precision, and to lean as near her warm shoulder as we dare to pour out for her the sacred wine.

Yes! for sure I was twenty again, for the performance of these simple services for Nicolete gave me a thrill of pure boyish pleasure such as I had never expected to feel again. And did she not make a knight of me by gently asking if I would be so kind as to carve the chicken, and how she laughed

quite disproportionally at my school-boy
story of the man who, being asked to carve a
pigeon, said he thought they had better send
for a wood-carver, as it seemed to be a wood
pigeon.

And while we ate and drank and laughed
and chatted, the books around us were weav-
ing their spells.   Even before the invention
of printing books were "love's purveyors."
Was it not a book that sent Paolo and
Francesca for ever wandering on that stormy
wind of passion and of death?   And nowadays the part played by books in human
drama is greater than we perhaps realise.
Apart from their serious influence as deter-
mining destinies of the character, what end-
less opportunities they afford to lovers, who
perhaps are denied all other meeting-places
than may be found on the tell-tale pages of
a marked volume.   The method is so easy
and so unsuspect.   You have only to put
faint pencil-marks against the tenderest
passages in your favourite new poet, and
lend the volume to Her, and She has only to
leave here and there the dropped violet of a
timid confirmatory initial, for you to know

your fate.   And what a touchstone books
thus become! Indeed they simplify love-
making, from every point of view.   With
books so inexpensive and accessible to all as
they are to-day, no one need run any risks
of marrying the wrong woman.   He has
only to put her through an unconscious
examination by getting her to read and mark
a few of his favourite authors, and he is thus
in possession of the master clues of her
character.   With a list of her month's reading and a photograph, a man ought to be
able to make up his mind about any given
woman, even though he has never spoken to
her.   "Name your favourite writer" should
be one of the first questions in the Engagement Catechism.

There is, indeed, no such short cut to
knowledge of each other as a talk about
books.   One short afternoon is enough for
any two book-lovers, though they may have
met for the first time in the morning, to
make up their minds whether or not they have
been born for each other.   If you are agreed,
say, in admiring Meredith, Hardy, Omar
Khayyam, and Maeterlinck, — to take four

particularly test-authors, — there is nothing to prevent your marrying at once. Indeed, a love for any one of these significant writers will be enough, not to speak of an admiration for "Aucassin and Nicolete."

Now, Nicolete and I soon found that we had all these and many another writer in common, and before our lunch was ended we were nearer to each other than many old friends. The heart does not more love the heart that loves it than the brain loves the brain that comprehends it; and, whatever else was to befall us, Nicolete and I were already in love with each other's brains. Whether or not the malady would spread till it reached the heart is the secret of some future chapter.

CHAPTER VI

A FAIRY TALE AND ITS FAIRY TAILORS

As this is not a realistic novel, I do not hold myself bound, as I have said before, to account reasonably for everything that is done — least of all, said — within its pages. I simply say, So it happened, or So it is, and expect the reader to take my word.   If he be uncivil enough to doubt it, we may as well stop playing this game of fancy.   It is one of the first conditions of enjoying a book, as it is of all successful hypnotism, that the reader surrenders up his will to the writer, who, of course, guarantees to return it to him at the close of the volume.   If you say that no young lady would have behaved as I have presently to relate of Nicolete, that no parents were ever so accommodating in the world of reality, I reply, — No doubt you are right, but none the less what I have to tell is true and really did happen, for all that.

And not only did it happen, but to the whimsically minded, to the true children of fancy, it will seem the most natural thing in the world. No doubt they will wonder why I have made such a preamble about it, as indeed, now I think of it, so do I.

Again I claim exemption in this wandering history from all such descriptive drudgery upon second, third, and fourth *dramatis personæ* as your thorough-going novelist must undertake with a good grace. Like a host and hostess at a reception, the poor novelist has to pretend to be interested in everybody, — in the dull as in the brilliant, in the bore as in the beauty. I'm afraid I should never do as a novelist, for I should waste all my time with the heroine; whereas the true novelist is expected to pay as much attention to the heroine's parents as though he were a suitor for her hand. Indeed, there is no relative of hero or heroine too humble or stupid for such a novelist as the great Balzac. He will invite the dullest of them to stay with him for quite prolonged visits, and without a murmur set apart a suite of chapters for their accommodation. I'm not sure that the humanity of the reader in these cases is of such comprehensive sympathy as the novelist's, and it may well be that the novelist undertakes all such hard labour under a misapprehension of the desires of the reader, who, as a rule, I fancy, is as anxious to join the ladies as the novelist himself.   Indeed, I believe that there is an opportunity for a new form of novel, in which the novelist, as well as the reader, will skip all the dull people, and merely indicate such of them as are necessary to the action by an outline or a symbol, compressing their familiar psychology, and necessary plot-interferences with the main characters, into recognised formulæ.   For the benefit of readers voracious for everything about everybody, schedule chapters might be provided by inferior novelists, good at painting say tiresome bourgeois fathers, gouty uncles and brothers in the army, as sometimes in great pictures we read that the sheep in the foreground have been painted by Mr. So-and-so, R. A.

The Major-General and his Lady were taking the waters at Wiesbaden.   That was all I knew of Nicolete's parents, and all I needed to know; with the exception of one good action, — at her urgent entreaty they had left Nicolete behind them, with no other safeguard than a charming young lady companion, whose fitness for her sacred duties consisted in a temperament hardly less romantic and whimsical than Nicolete's own. She was too charming to deserve the name of obstacle; and as there was no other —

But I admit that the cart has got a little in front of the horse, and I grow suddenly alarmed lest the reader should be suspecting me of an elopement, or some such romantic vulgarity. If he will only put any such thoughts from his mind, I promise to proceed with the story in a brief and business-like manner forthwith.

We are back once more at the close of the last chapter, in Nicolete's book-bower in the wildwood. It is an hour or two later, and the afternoon sun is flooding with a searching glory all the secret places of the woodland. Hidden nooks and corners, un-used to observation, suddenly gleam and blush in effulgent exposure, — like lovers whom the unexpected turning on of a light

has revealed kissing in the dark, — and are
as suddenly, unlike the lovers, left in their
native shade again.   It was that rich afternoon sunlight that loves to flash into teacups
as though they were crocuses, that loves to
run a golden finger along the beautiful
wrinkles of old faces and light up the noble
hollows of age-worn eyes; the sunlight that
loves to fall with transfiguring beam on the
once dear book we never read, or, with ma-
licious inquisitiveness, expose to undreamed-
of detection the undusted picture, or the gold-
dusted legs of remote chairs, which the poor
housemaid has forgotten.

So in Nicolete's bower it illuminated with
strange radiancy the dainty disorder of
deserted lunch, made prisms out of the
wine-glasses, painted the white cloth with
wedge-shaped rainbows, and flooded the cav-
ernous interiors of the half-eaten fowl with
a pathetic yellow torchlight.

Leaving that melancholy relic of carnivorous appetite, it turned its bold gold gaze
on Nicolete.   No need to transfigure her!
But, heavens! how grandly her young face
took the great kiss of the god!   Then it fell

for a tender moment on the jaundiced page
of my old Boccaccio, — a rare edition, which
I had taken from my knapsack to indulge
myself with the appreciation of a connois-
seur. Next minute "the unobstructed beam"
was shining right into the knapsack itself,
for all the world like one of those little
demon electric lights with which the dentist
makes a momentary treasure-cave of your distended jaws, flashing with startled stalactite.
At the same moment Nicolete's starry eyes
took the same direction; then there broke
from her her lovely laughter, merry and
inextinguishable.

Once more, need I say, my petticoat had
played me false — or should I not say true?
For there was its luxurious lace border, a
thing for the soft light of the boudoir, or the
secret moonlight of love's permitted eyes,
alone to see, shamelessly brazening it out in
this terrible sunlight.   Obviously there was
but one way out of the dilemma, to confess
my pilgrimage to Nicolete, and reveal to
her all the fanciful absurdity to which, after
all, I owed the sight of her.

"So that is why you pleaded so hard for

that poor trout," she said, when I had finished. "Well, you are a fairy prince indeed!
Now, do you know what the punishment of
your nonsense is to be?"

"Is it very severe and humiliating?" I
asked.

"You must judge of that. It is — to take
me with you!"

"You, — what do you mean?"

"Yes, — not for good and all, of course,
but just for, say, a fortnight, just a fortnight
of rambles and adventures, and then to de-
liver me safe home again where you found
me — "

"But it is impossible," I almost gasped
in surprise. "Of course you are not
serious?"

"I am, really, and you will take me,
won't you?" she continued pleadingly.
"You don't know how we women envy you
men those wonderful walking-tours we can
only read about in Hazlitt or Stevenson.
We are not allowed to move without a nurse
or a footman. From the day we are born
to the day we die, we are never left a
moment to ourselves. But you — you can

go out into the world, the mysterious world, do as you will, go where you will, wander here, wander there, follow any bye-way that takes your fancy, put up at old inns, make strange acquaintances, have all kinds of romantic experiences — Oh, to be a man for a fortnight, your younger brother for a fortnight!"

"It is impossible!" I repeated.

"It isn't at all," she persisted, with a fine blush. "If you will only be nice and kind, and help me to some Rosalind's clothes. You have only to write to your tailors, or send home for a spare suit of clothes, — with a little managing yours would just fit me, you're not so much taller, — and then we could start, like two comrades, seeking adventures. Oh, how glorious it would be!"

It was in vain that I brought the batteries of common-sense to bear upon her whim. I raised every possible objection in vain.

I pointed out the practical difficulties. There were her parents. Weren't they drinking the waters at Wiesbaden, and weren't they to go on drinking them for

another three weeks? My fancy made a
picture of them distended with three weeks'
absorption of mineral springs. Then there
was her companion. Nicolete was confident
of her assistance. Then I tried vilifying
myself. How could she run the risk of
trusting herself to such intimate companionship with a man whom she had n't known
half a dozen hours? This she laughed to
scorn. Presently I was silent from sheer
lack of further objections; and need I say
that all the while there had been a traitor
impulse in my heart, a weak sweetness urg-
ing me on to accept the pretty chance which
the good genius of my pilgrimage had so evidently put in my way, — for, after all, what
harm could it do? With me Nicolete was,
indeed, safe, — that, of course, I knew, —
and safely she should come back home again
after her little frolic. All that was true
enough. And how charming it would be to
have such a dainty companion! then the
fun, the fancy, the whim of it all. What
was the use of setting out to seek adventures
if I did n't pursue them when found.

Well, the long and short of it was that I

agreed to undertake the adventure, provided that Nicolete could win over the lady whom at the beginning of the chapter I declared too charming to be described as an obstacle.

By nine o'clock the following morning the fairy tailors, as Nicolete called them, were at work on the fairy clothes, and, at the end of three days, there came by parcel-post a bulky unromantic-looking brown-paper parcel, which it was my business to convey to Nicolete under cover of the dark.

CHAPTER VII

FROM THE MORNING STAR TO THE MOON

I QUITE realise that this book is written perhaps only just in time for the motive of these two or three chapters to be appreciated in its ancient piquancy. Very soon, alas! the sexes will be robbed of one of the first and most thrilling motives of romance, the motive of *As You Like It*, the romance of wearing each other's clothes. Alas, that every advance of reason should mean a corresponding retreat of romance! It is only reasonable that woman, being — have you yet realised the fact? — a biped like her brothers, should, when she takes to her brothers' recreations, dress as those recreations demand; and yet the death of Rosalind is a heavy price to pay for the lady bicyclist. So soon as the two sexes wear the same clothes, they may as well wear nothing; the game of sex is up.   In this matter, as in others, we cannot both have our cake and eat it.   All romance, like all temptation, is founded on the Fascination of the Exception.   So soon as the exception becomes, instead of merely proving, the rule, that particular avenue of romance is closed.   The New Woman of the future will be the woman with the petticoats, she who shall restore the ancient Eleusinian mysteries of the silk skirt and the tea-gown.

Happily for me, my acquaintance among the Rosalinds of the bicycle, at this period of my life, was but slight, and thus no familiarity with the tweed knickerbocker feminine took off the edge of my delight on first beholding Nicolete clothed in like manhood with ourselves, and yet, delicious paradox! looking more like a woman than ever.

During those three days while the fairy tailors were at work our friendship had not been idle.   Indeed, some part of each day we had spent diligently learning each other, as travellers to distant lands across the Channel work hard at phrase-book and Baedeker the week before their departure.

Meanwhile too I had made the acquaintance of the charming lady Obstacle, — as it proved so unfair to call her,—and by some process of natural magnetism we had immediately won each other's hearts, so that on the moonlight night on which I took the river path with my brown-paper parcel there was no misgiving in my heart, — nothing but harping and singing, and blessings on the river that seemed all silver with the backs of magic trout. As I thought of all I owed that noble fish, I kneeled by the river's bearded lip, among the nettles and the meadow-sweet, and swore by the inconstant moon that trout and I were henceforth kinsmen, and that between our houses should be an eternal amity. The chub and the dace and the carp, not to speak of that Chinese pirate the pike, might still look to it, when I came forth armed with rod and line; but for me and my house the trout is henceforth sacred. By the memory of the Blessed Saint Izaak, I swore it !

My arrival at Beaucaire was one of great excitement. Nicolete and the Obstacle were both awaiting me, for the mysteries of mas-

culine attire were not to be explored alone.
The parcel was snatched quite unceremoni-
ously from my hands, the door shut upon
me, and I laughingly bidden go listen to
the nightingale.   I was not long in finding
one, nor, being an industrious phrase-maker,
did I waste my time, for, before I was summoned to behold Nicolete in all her boyhood,
I had found occasion and moonlight to
remark to my pocket-book that, *Though all
the world has heard the song of the Nightingale to the Rose, only the Nightingale has
heard the answer of the Rose*.   This I hurriedly hid in my heart for future conversation, as the pre-arranged tinkle of the silver
bell called me to the rose.

Would, indeed, that I were a nightingale
to sing aright the beauty of that rose with
which, think of it, I was to spend a whole
fortnight, — yes, no less than fourteen wonderful days.

The two girls were evidently proud of
themselves at having succeeded so well with
the mysterious garments.   There were one
or two points on which they needed my
guidance, but they were unimportant; and

when at last Nicolete would consent to stand up straight and let me have a good look at her, — for, poor child! she was as shy and shrinking as though she had nothing on, — she made a very pretty young man indeed.

She did n't, I 'm afraid, look like a young man of our degenerate day. She was far too beautiful and distinguished for that. Besides, her dark curling hair, quite short for a woman, was too long, and her eyes — like the eyes of all poets — were women's eyes. She looked, indeed, like one of those wonderful boys of the Italian Renaissance, whom you may still see at the National Gallery, whose beauty is no denial, but rather the stamp of their slender, supple strength, young painters and sculptors who held the palette for Leonardo, or wielded the chisel for Michelangelo, and anon threw both aside to take up sword for Guelf or Ghibelline in the narrow streets of Florence.

Her knapsack was already packed, and its contents included a serge skirt "in case of emergencies." Already, she naughtily reminded me, we possessed a petticoat between us.

The brief remainder of the evening passed in excited chatter and cigarettes, and in my instructing Nicolete in certain tricks of masculine deportment.   The chief difficulty I hardly like mentioning; and if the Obstacle had not been present, I certainly dare not have spoken of it to Nicolete.   I mean that she was so shy about her pretty legs.   She could n't cross them with any successful nonchalance.

"You must take your legs more for granted, dear Nicolete," I summoned courage to say.   "The nonchalance of the legs is the first lesson to be learnt in such a masquerade as this.   You must regard them as so much bone and iron, rude skeleton joints and shins, as though they were the bones of the great elk or other extinct South Kensington specimen," — "not," I added in my heart, "as the velvet and ivory which they are."

We had agreed to start with the sun on the morrow, so as to get clear of possible Peeping Toms; and when good-nights had been said, and I was once more swinging towards my inn, it seemed but an hour or

two, as indeed it was, before I heard four
o'clock drowsily announced through my
bedroom door, and before I was once more
striding along that river-bank all dew-
silvered with last night's moonlight, the
sun rubbing his great eye on the horizon,
the whole world yawning through dainty
bed-clothes of mist, and here and there a
copse-full of birds congratulating themselves
on their early rising.

Nicolete was not quite ready, so I had to go
listen to the lark, about whom, alas! I could
find nothing to say to my pocket-book, before
Nicolete, armed *cap-à-pie* with stick and
knapsack, appeared at the door of her châlet.

The Obstacle was there to see us start.
She and Nicolete exchanged many kisses
which were hard to bear, and the first quarter
of an hour of our journey was much obstructed
by the farewells of her far-fluttering handkerchief. When at last we were really
alone, I turned and looked at Nicolete striding manfully at my side, just to make sure
that it was really true.

"Well, we're in for it now," I said;
"aren't you frightened?"

"Oh, it's wonderful," she replied; "don't spoil it by talking."

And I did n't; for who could hope to compete with the sun, who was making the whole dewy world shake with laughter at his brilliancy, or with the birds, any one of whom was a poet at least equal to Herrick?

Presently we found ourselves at four cross-roads, with a four-fingered post in the centre. We had agreed to leave our destination to chance.   We read the sign-post.

"Which shall we choose?" I said, —

> "Aucassin, true love and fair,
>   To what land do we repair?"

"Don't you think this one," she replied. "this one? — *To the Moon!*"

"Certainly, we could n't find a prettier place; but it's a long way," I replied, looking up at the sky, all roses and pearls, — "a long way from the Morning Star to the Moon."

"All the longer to be free," cried Nicolete, recklessly.

"So be it," I assented.   "*Allons* — to the Moon!"

CHAPTER VIII

THE KIND OF THING THAT HAPPENS IN THE MOON

Two friends of my youth, with whom it would be hopeless to attempt competition, have described the star-strewn journey to the moon. It is not for me to essay again where the ingenious M. Jules Verne and Mr. William Morris have preceded me. Besides, the journey is nowadays much more usual, and therefore much less adventurous, than when those revered writers first described it. In the middle ages a journey to the moon with a woman you loved was a very perilous matter indeed. Even in the last century the roads were much beset with danger; but in our own day, like most journeys, it is accomplished with ease and safety in a few hours.

However, to the latter-day hero, whose appetite for dragons is not keen, this absence

of adventure is perhaps rather pleasurable
than otherwise; and I confess that I enjoyed
the days I spent on foot with Nicolete none
the less because they passed in tranquil
uneventfulness, — that is, without events of
the violent kind.   Of course, all depends on
what you call an event.   We were not way-
laid by robbers, we fed and slept unchal-
lenged at inns, we escaped collision with
the police, and we encountered no bodily
dangers of any kind; yet should I not call
the journey uneventful, nor indeed, I think,
would Nicolete.

To me it was one prolonged divine event,
and, with such daily intercourse with Nicolete, I never dreamed of craving for any
other excitement.   To walk from morning
to evening by her side, to minister to her
moods, to provide such entertainment as I
might for her brain, and watch like a father
over her physical needs; to note when she
was weary and too proud to show it, and to
pretend to be done up myself; to choose for
her the easiest path, and keep my eyes open
for wayside flowers and every country surprise, — these, and a hundred other atten-

tions, kept my heart and mind in busy service.

To picnic by some lonely stream-side on a few sandwiches, a flask of claret, and a pennyworth of apples; to talk about the books we loved; to exchange our hopes and dreams, — we asked nothing better than this simple fare.

And so a week went by. But, though so little had seemed to happen, and though our walking record was shamefully modest, yet, imperceptible as the transition had been, we were, quite insensibly indeed, and unacknowledged, in a very different relation to each other than when we had started out from the Morning Star. In fact, to make no more words about it, I was head over heels in love with Nicolete, and I think, without conceit, I may say that Nicolete was rapidly growing rather fond of me. Apart from anything else, we were such excellent chums. We got along together as if indeed we had been two brothers, equable in our tempers and one in our desires.

At last the feeling on my side became so importunate that I could no longer keep silence.

We were seated together taking tea at a small lonely inn, whose windows looked out over a romantic little lake, backed by Salvator Rosa pine-woods. The sun was beginning to grow dreamy, and the whole world to wear a dangerously sentimental expression.

I forget exactly what it was, but something in our talk had set us glowing, had touched tender chords of unexpected sympathy, and involuntarily I stretched out my hand across the corner of the table and pressed Nicolete's hand as it rested on the cloth. She did not withdraw it, and our eyes met with a steady gaze of love.

"Nicolete," I said presently, when I could speak, "it is time for you to be going back home."

"Why?" she asked breathlessly.

"Because," I answered, "I must love you if you stay."

"Would you then bid me go?" she said.

"Nicolete," I said, "don't tempt me. Be a good girl and go home."

"But supposing I don't want to go home," she said; "supposing — oh, supposing I love you too? Would you still bid me go?"

"Yes," I said. "In that case it would be even more imperative."

"Aucassin!"

"It is true, it is true, dear Nicolete."

"Then, Aucassin," she replied, almost sternly, in her great girlish love, "this is true also, — I love you. I have never loved, shall never love, any man but you!"

"Nicolete!"

"Aucassin!"

There were no more words spoken between us for a full hour that afternoon.

CHAPTER IX

WRITTEN BY MOONLIGHT

I KNEW deep down in my heart that it could n't last, yet how deny myself these roses, while the opportunity of gathering them was mine! — the more so, as I believed it would do no harm to Nicolete. At all events, a day or two more or less of moonshine would make no matter either way. And so all next day we walked hand in hand through Paradise.

It has been said by them of old time, and our fathers have told us, that the kiss of first love, the first kiss of the first woman we love, is beyond all kisses sweet; and true it is. But true is it also that no less sweet is the first kiss of the last woman we love.

Putting my faith in old saws, as a young man will, I had never dreamed to know again a bliss so divinely passionate and pure as came to me with every glance of Nicolete's sweet eyes, with every simple pressure of her hand; and the joy that was mine when sometimes, stopping on our way, we would press together our lips ever so gravely and tenderly, seems too holy even to speak of.

The holy angels could not have loved Nicolete with a purer love, a love freer from taint of any earthly thought, than I, a man of thirty, *blasé*, and fed from my youth upon the honeycomb of woman.

It was curious that the first difficulty of our pilgrimage should befall us the very next day. Coming towards nightfall to a small inn in a lonely unpopulated country-side, we found that the only accommodation the inn afforded was one double-bedded room, and there was no other inn for at least ten miles. I think I was more troubled than Nicolete. When, after interviewing the landlady, I came and told her of the dilemma, where she sat in the little parlour wearied out with the day's walk, she blushed, it is true, but seemed little put about. Indeed, she laughed, and said it was rather fun, "like something out of Sterne,"

— of such comfort is a literary reference in all seasons and circumstances, — and then she added, with a sweet look that sent the blood rioting about my heart, "It won't matter so much, will it, love, *now ?*"

There proved nothing for it but to accept the situation, and we made the arrangement that Nicolete was to slip off to bed first, and then put out the light and go to sleep. However, when I followed her, having sat up as long as the landlady's patience would endure, I found that, though she had blown out the candle, she had forgotten to put out the moon, which shone as though it were St. Agnes' Eve across half the room.

I stole in very shyly, kept my eyes sternly from Nicolete's white bed, though, as I could n't shut my ears, the sound of her breathing came to me with indescribable sweetness. After I had lain among the sheets some five or ten minutes, I was suddenly startled by a little voice within the room saying, —

"I 'm not asleep."

"Well, you should be, naughty child.

Now shut your eyes and go to sleep, — and fair dreams and sweet repose," I replied.

"Won't you give me one little good-night kiss?"

"I gave you one downstairs."

"Is it very wicked to want another?"

There was not a foot between our two beds, so I bent over and took her soft white shoulders in my arms and kissed her. All the heaped-up sweetness of the whitest, freshest flowers of the spring seemed in my embrace as I kissed her, so soft, so fragrant, so pure; and as the moonlight was the white fire in our blood. Softly I released her, stroked her brown hair, and turned again to my pillow. Presently the little voice was in the room again, —

"May n't I hold your hand? Somehow I feel lonely and frightened."

So our hands made a bridge across which our dreams might pass through the night, and after a little while I knew that she slept.

As I lay thus holding her hand, and listening to her quiet breathing, I realised once more what my young Alastor had meant by

the purity of high passion.   For indeed the
moonlight that fell across her bosom was
not whiter than my thoughts, nor could any
kiss — were it even such a kiss as Venus
promised to the betrayer of Psyche — even
in its fiercest delirium, be other than dross
compared with the wild white peace of those
silent hours when we lay thus married and
maiden side by side.

CHAPTER X

HOW ONE MAKES LOVE AT THIRTY

My sleeplessness while Nicolete slept had not been all ecstasy, for I had come to a bitter resolution; and next morning, when we were once more on our way, I took a favourable opportunity of conveying it to Nicolete.

"Nicolete," I said, as we rested awhile by the roadside, "I have something serious to say to you."

"Yes, dear," she said, looking rather frightened.

"Well, dear, it is this, — our love must end with our holiday. No good can come of it."

"But oh, why? I love you."

"Yes, and I love you, — love you as I never thought I could love again. Yet I know it is all a dangerous dream, — a trick of our brains, an illusion of our tastes."

"But oh, why? I love you."

"Yes, you do to-day, I know; but it could n't last. I believe I could love you for ever; but even so, it would n't be right. You could n't go on loving me. I am too old, too tired, too *désillusioné*, perhaps too selfish."

"I will love you always!" said girl Nicolete.

"Whereas you," I continued, disregarding the lovely refrain of her tear-choked voice, "are standing on the wonderful threshold of life, waiting in dreamland for the dawn. And it will come, and with it the fairy prince, with whom you shall wander hand in hand through all its fairy rose-gardens; but I, dear Nicolete, — I am not he."

Nicolete did not speak.

"I know," I continued, pressing her hand, "that I may seem young enough to talk like this, but some of us get through life quicker than others, and when we say, ' It is done,' it is no use for onlookers to say, ' Why, it is just beginning!' Believe me, Nicolete, I am not fit husband for you."

"Then shall I take no other," said Nicolete, with set face.

"Oh, yes, you will," I rejoined; "let but a month or two pass, and you will see how wise I was, after all. Besides, there are other reasons, of which there is no need to speak —"

"What reasons?"

"Well," I said, half laughing, "there is the danger that, after all, we might n't agree. There is nothing so perilously difficult as the daily intercourse of two people who love each other. You are too young to realise its danger. And I could n't bear to see our love worn away by the daily dropping of tears, not to speak of its being rent by the dynamite of daily quarrels. We know each other's tastes, but we know hardly anything of each other's natures."

Nicolete looked at me strangely. 'Troth, it was a strange way to make love, I knew.

"And what else?" she asked somewhat coldly.

"Well, then, though it 's not a thing one cares to speak of, I 'm a poor man —"

Nicolete broke through my sentence with a scornful exclamation.

"You," I continued straight on, — "well,

you have been accustomed to a certain spaciousness and luxury of life. This it would be out of my power to continue for you. These are real reasons, very real reasons, dear Nicolete, though you may not think so now. The law of the world in these matters is very right. For the rich and the poor to marry is to risk, terribly risk, the very thing they would marry for — their love. Love is better an unmarried than a married regret."

Nicolete was silent again.

"Think of your little woodland châlet, and your great old trees in the park, — you could n't live without them. I have, at most, but one tree worth speaking of to offer you — "

I purposely waived the glamour which my old garden had for my mind, and which I would n't have exchanged for fifty parks.

"Trees!" retorted Nicolete, — "what are trees?"

"Ah, my dear girl, they are a good deal, — particularly when they are genealogical, as my one tree is not."

"Aucassin," she said suddenly, almost

fiercely, "can you really jest? Tell me
this, — do you love me?"

"I love you," I said simply; "and it is
just because I love you so much that I have
talked as I have done. No man situated
as I am who loved you could have talked
otherwise."

"Well, I have heard it all, weighed it
all," said Nicolete, presently; "and to me it
is but as thistledown against the love within
my heart. Will you cast away a woman
who loves you for theories? You know you
love me, know I love you. We should have
our trials, our ups and downs, I know; but
surely it is by those that true love learns how
to grow more true and strong. Oh, I cannot
argue! Tell me again, do you love me?"

And there she broke down and fell sobbing into my arms. I consoled her as best
I might, and presently she looked up at me
through her tears.

"Tell me again," she said, "that you love
me, just as you did yesterday, and promise
never to speak of all those cruel things
again. Ah! have you thought of the kind
of men you would give me up to?"

At that I confess I shuddered, and I gave her the required assurance.

"And you won't be wise and reasonable and ridiculous any more?"

"No," I answered; adding in my mind, "not, at all events, for the present."

CHAPTER XI

HOW ONE PLAYS THE HERO AT THIRTY

HAD we only been able to see a day into the future, we might have spared ourselves this agonising, for all our doubts and fears were suddenly dispersed in an entirely unexpected manner. Happily these interior problems are not infrequently resolved by quite exterior forces.

We were sitting the following afternoon in one of those broad bay windows such as one finds still in some old country inns, just thinking about starting once more on our way, when suddenly Nicolete, who had been gazing out idly into the road, gave a little cry. I followed her glance. A carriage with arms on its panels had stopped at the inn, and as a smart footman opened the door, a fine grey-headed military-looking man stepped out and strode hurriedly up the inn steps.

"Aucassin," gasped Nicolete, "it is my father!"

It was too true. The old man's keen eye had caught sight of Nicolete at the window also, and in another moment we were all three face to face. I must do the Major-General the justice of saying that he made as little of a "scene" of it as possible.

"Now, my girl," he said, "I have come to put an end to this nonsense. Have you a petticoat with you? Well, go upstairs and get it on. I will wait for you here . . . On you, sir, I shall waste no words. From what I have heard, you are as moonstruck as my daughter."

"Of course," I stammered, "I cannot expect you to understand the situation, though I think, if you would allow me, I could in a very few words make it somewhat clearer, — make you realise that, after all, it has been a very innocent and childish escapade, in which there has been no harm and a great deal of pleasure — "

But the Major-General cut me short.

"I should prefer," he said, "not to discuss the matter. I may say that I realise that my daughter has been safe in your hands, however foolish," — for this I thanked him with a bow, — "but I must add that your eccentric acquaintance must end here — "

I said him neither yea nor nay; and while we stood in armed and embarrassed silence, Nicolete appeared with white face at the door, clothed in her emergency petticoat. Alas! it was for no such emergency as this that it had been destined that merry night when she had packed it in her knapsack. With a stern bow her father turned from me to join her; but she suddenly slipped past him, threw her arms round me, and kissed me one long passionate kiss.

"Aucassin, be true," she cried, "I will never forget you, — no one shall come between us;" and then bursting into tears, she buried her face in her hands and followed her father from the room.

In another moment she had been driven away, and I sat as one stupefied in the inn window. But a few short minutes ago she had been sitting merrily prattling by my side, and now I was once more as lonely as if we had never met. Presently I became conscious in my reverie of a little crumpled piece of paper on the floor. I picked it up. It was a little note pencilled in her bedroom at the last moment. "Aucassin," it ran, just like her last passionate words, "be true. I will never forget you. Stay here till I write to you, and oh, write to me soon!— Your broken-hearted Nicolete."

As I read, I saw her lovely young face, radiant with love and sorrow as I had last seen it, and pressing the precious little letter to my lips, I said fervently, "Yes, Nicolete, I will be true."

CHAPTER XII

IN WHICH I REVIEW MY ACTIONS AND RENEW MY RESOLUTIONS

No doubt the youthful reader will have but a poor opinion of me after the last two chapters. He will think that in the scene with the Major-General I acted with lamentably little spirit, and that generally my friend Alastor would have proved infinitely more worthy of the situation. It is quite true, I confess it. The whole episode was made for Alastor. Nicolete and he were born for each other. Alas! it is one of the many drawbacks of experience that it frequently prevents our behaving with spirit.

I must be content to appeal to the wiser and therefore sadder reader, of whom I have but a poor opinion if he too fails to understand me. He, I think, will understand why I didn't promptly assault the Major-General, seize Nicolete by the waist, thrust

her into her ancestral carriage, haul the
coachman from his box, and, seizing the
reins, drive away in triumph before aston-
ishment had time to change into pursuit.
Truly it had been but the work of a moment,
and there was only one consideration which
prevented my following this now-I-call-that-
heroic course. It is a consideration I dare
hardly venture to write, and the confession
of which will, I know, necessitate my changing my age back again to thirty on the
instant. Oh, be merciful, dear romantic
reader! I didn't strike the Major-General,
because, oh, because *I agreed with him!*

I loved Nicolete, you must have felt that.
She was sweet to me as the bunch of white
flowers that, in their frail Venetian vase, stand
so daintily on my old bureau as I write,
doing their best to sweeten my thoughts.
Dear was she to me as the birds that out in
the old garden yonder sing and sing their
best to lift up my leaden heart. She was
dear as the Spring itself, she was only less
dear than Autumn.

Yes, black confession! after the first
passion of her loss, the immediate ache of

her young beauty had passed, and I was able
to analyse what I really felt, I not only
agreed with him, I thanked God for the
Major-General! He had saved me from
playing the terrible part of executioner.
He had just come in time to behead the
Lady Jane Grey of our dreams.

I should have no qualms about tightening
the rope round the neck of some human
monster, or sticking a neat dagger or bullet
into a dangerous, treacherous foe, but to kill
a dream is a sickening business. It goes on
moaning in such a heart-breaking fashion,
and you never know when it is dead. All
on a sudden some night it will come wailing
in the wind outside your window, and you
must blacken your heart and harden your
face with another strangling grip of its slim
appealing throat, another blow upon its
angel eyes. Even then it will recover, and
you will go on being a murderer, making
for yourself day by day a murderer's face,
without the satisfaction of having really
murdered.

But what of Nicolete? do you exclaim.
Have you no thought for her, bleeding her

heart away in solitude? Can you so soon
forget those appealing eyes? Yes, I have
thought for her. Would God that I could
bear for her those growing pains of the
heart! and I shall never forget those farewell eyes. But then, you see, I had firmly
realised this, that she would sooner recover
from our separation than from our marriage;
that her love for me, pretty and poignant
and dramatic while it lasted, was a book-
born, book-fed dream, which must die soon
or late,—the sooner the better for the peace
of the dreams that in the course of nature
would soon spring up to take its place.

But while I realised all this, and, with
a veritable aching of the heart at the loss
of her, felt a curious satisfaction at the turn
of events, still my own psychology became
all the more a puzzle to me, and I asked myself, with some impatience, what I would be
at, and what it was I really wanted.

Here had I but a few moments ago been
holding in my hands the very dream I had
set out to find, and here was I secretly
rejoicing to be robbed of it! If Nicolete
did not fulfil the conditions of that mysti-

cal Golden Girl, in professed search for whom I had set out that spring morning, well, the good genius of my pilgrimage felt it time to resign. Better give it up at once, and go back to my books and my bachelor-hood, if I were so difficult to please. No wonder my kind providence felt provoked. It had provided me with the sweetest pink-and-porcelain dream of a girl, and might reasonably have concluded that his labours on my behalf were at an end.

But, really, there is no need to lecture me upon the charms and virtues of Nicolete, for I loved them from the first moment of our strange introduction, and I dream of them still. There was indeed only one quality of womanhood in which she was lack-ing, and in which, after much serious self-examination, I discovered the reason of my instinctive self-sacrifice of her, — *she had never suffered.* As my heart had warned me at the beginning, "she was hoping too much from life to spend one's days with." She lacked the subtle half-tones of experience. She lacked all that a pretty wrinkle or two might have given. There was no shadowy melancholy in her sky-clear eyes. She was gay indeed, and had a certain childish humour; but she had none of that humour which comes of the resigned perception that the world is out of joint, and that you were never born to set it right. These characteristics I had yet to find in woman. There was still, therefore, an object to my quest. Indeed my experience had provided me with a formula. I was in search of a woman who, in addition to every other feminine charm and virtue, was a woman who had suffered.

With this prayer I turned once more to the genius of my pilgrimage. "Grant me," I asked, "but this — *A Woman who has suffered!*" and, apparently as a consequence, he became once more quite genial. He seemed to mean that a prayer so easy to grant would put any god into a good temper; and possibly he smiled with a deeper meaning too.

BOOK III

CHAPTER I

IN WHICH I RETURN TO MY RIGHT AGE AND ENCOUNTER A COMMON OBJECT OF THE COUNTRY

AND so when the days of my mourning for Nicolete were ended (and in this sentence I pass over letters to and fro, — letters wild from Nicolete, letters wise from Aucassin, letters explanatory and apologetic from the Obstacle — how the Major-General had suddenly come home quite unexpectedly and compelled her to explain Nicolete's absence, etc., etc. Dear Obstacle! I should rather have enjoyed a pilgrimage with her too) — I found myself one afternoon again upon the road. The day had been very warm and dusty, and had turned sleepy towards tea-time.

I had now pretty clearly in my mind what I wanted. This time it was, all other things equal, to be "a woman who had suffered," and to this end, I had, before starting out once more, changed my age back again at the inn and written "Aetat. 30" after my name in the visitors' book. As a young man I was an evident failure, and so, having made the countersign, I was speedily transformed to my old self; and I must say that it was a most comfortable feeling, something like getting back again into an old coat or an old pair of shoes. I never wanted to be young again as long as I lived. Youth was too much like the Sunday clothes of one's boyhood. Moreover, I had a secret conviction that the woman I was now in search of would prefer one who had had some experience at being a man, who would bring her not the green plums of his love, but the cunningly ripened nectarines, a man to whom love was something of an art as well as an inspiration.

It was in this frame of mind that I came upon the following scene.

The lane was a very cloistral one, with a ribbon of gravelly road, bordered on each side with a rich margin of turf and a scramble

12

of blackberry bushes, green turf banks and
dwarf oak-trees making a rich and plenteous
shade.   My attention was caught firstly by
a bicycle lying carelessly on the turf, and
secondly and lastly by a graceful woman's
figure, recumbent and evidently sleeping
against the turf bank, well tucked in among
the afternoon shadows.   My coming had not
aroused her, and so I stole nearer to her on
tiptoe.

She was a pretty woman, of a striking modern type, tall, well-proportioned,
strong, I should say, with a good complexion
that had evidently been made just a little
better.   But her most striking feature was
an opulent mass of dark red hair, which had
fallen in some disorder and made quite a
pillow for her head.   Her hat was off, lying
in its veil by her side, and a certain general
abandon of her figure, — which was clothed
in a short cloth skirt, cut with that unmistakable touch which we call style — betokened
weariness that could no longer wait for rest.

Poor child! she was tired out.   She must
never be left to sleep on there, for she
seemed good to sleep till midnight.

I turned to her bicycle, and, examining it with the air of a man who had won silver cups in his day, I speedily discovered what had been the mischief. The tire of the front wheel had been pierced, and a great thorn was protruding from the place. Evidently this had been too much for poor Rosalind, and it was not unlikely that she had cried herself to sleep.

I bent over her to look — yes, there were traces of tears. Poor thing! Then I had a kindly human impulse. I would mend the tire, having attended ambulance classes, do it very quietly so that she would n't hear, like the fairy cobblers who used to mend people's boots while they slept, and then wait in ambush to watch the effect upon her when she awoke.

What do you think of the idea?

But one important detail I have omitted from my description of the sleeper. Her left hand lay gloveless, and of the four rings on her third finger one was a wedding-ring.

"Such red hair, — and a wedding-ring!" I exclaimed inwardly. "How this woman must have suffered!"

CHAPTER II

MOVING the bicycle a little away, so that
my operations upon it might not arouse her,
I had soon made all right again, and when I
laid it once more where she had left it, she
was still sleeping as sound as ever. She
had only to sleep long enough, a sly thought
suggested, to necessitate her ending her
day's journey at the same inn as myself,
some five miles on the road. One virtue at
least the reader will allow to this history,
— we are seldom far away from an inn in its
pages. When I thought of that I sat stiller
than ever, hardly daring to turn over the
pages of Apuleius, which I had taken from
my knapsack to beguile the time, and, I
confess, to give my eyes some other occupation than the dangerous one of gazing

upon her face, dangerous in more ways
than one, but particularly dangerous at the
moment, because, as everybody knows, a
steady gaze on a sleeping face is apt to
awake the sleeper.   And she was n't to be
disturbed!

"No! she must n't waken before seven at
the latest," I said to myself, holding my
breath and starting in terror at every noise.
Once a great noisy bee was within an ace of
waking her, but I caught him with inspired
dexterity, and he buzzed around her head no
more.

But despite the providential loneliness of
the road, there were one or two terrors that
could not be disposed of so summarily.
The worst of all was a heavy miller's cart
which one could hardly crush to silence in
one's handkerchief; but it went so slowly,
and both man and horses were so sleepy,
that they passed unheard and unnoticing.

A sprightly tramp promised greater difficulty, and nothing but some ferocious pan-
tomime and a shilling persuaded him to
forego a choice fantasia of cockney humour.

A poor tired Italian organ-grinder, tramping with an equally tired monkey along the dusty roads, had to be bought off in a similar manner,— though he only cost sixpence. He gave me a Southern smile and shrug of comprehension, as one acquainted with affairs of the heart, — which was a relief after the cockney tramp's impudent expression of, no doubt, a precisely similar sentiment.

And then at last, just as my watch pointed to 6. 50 (how well I remember the exact moment!) Rosalind awoke suddenly, as women and children do, sitting straight up on the instant, and putting up her hands to her tousled hair, with a half-startled "Where am I?" When her hair was once more "respectable," she gave her skirts a shake, bent sideways to pull up her stockings and tighten her garters, looked at her watch, and then with an exclamation at the lateness of the hour, went over, with an air of desperate determination, to her bicycle.

"Now for this horrid puncture!" were the first words I was to hear fall from her lips.

She sought for the wound in the india-rubber with growing bewilderment.

"Goodness!" was her next exclamation, "why, there's nothing wrong with it.   Can I have been dreaming?"

"I hope your dreams have been pleasanter than that," I ventured at this moment to stammer, rising, a startling apparition, from my ambush behind a mound of brambles; and before she had time to take in the situation I added that I hoped she'd excuse my little pleasantry, and told her how I had noticed her and the wounded bicycle, et cetera, et cetera, as the reader can well imagine, without giving me the trouble of writing it all out.

She was sweetness itself on the instant.

"Excuse you!" she said, "I should think so.   Who wouldn't?   You can't tell the load you've taken off my mind.   I'm sure I must have groaned in my sleep — for I confess I cried myself to sleep over it."

"I thought so," I said with gravity, and eyes that didn't dare to smile outright till they had permission, which, however, was not long withheld them.

"How did you know?"

"Oh, intuition, of course — who wouldn't

have cried themselves to sleep, and so tired too ! "

" You're a nice sympathetic man, any-how," she laughed ; " what a pity you don't bicycle ! "

" Yes," I said, " I would give a thousand pounds for a bicycle at this moment."

" You ought to get a good one for that," she laughed, — " all bright parts nickel, I suppose ; indeed, you should get a real silver frame and gold handle-bars for that, don't you think? Well, it would be nice all the same to have your company a few miles, especially as it's growing dark," she added.

" Especially as it's growing dark," I re-peated.

" You won't be going much farther to-night. Have you fixed on your inn? " I continued innocently. She had — but that was in a town too far to reach to-night, after her long sleep.

" You might have wakened me," she said.

" Yes, it was stupid of me not to have thought of it," I answered, offering no expla-nation of the dead bee which at the moment I espied a little away in the grass, and saying nothing of the merry tramp and the melancholy musician.

Then we talked inns, and thus she fell beautifully into the pit which I had digged for her; and it was presently arranged that she should ride on to the Wheel of Pleasure and order a dinner, which she was to do me the honour of sharing with me.

I was to follow on foot as speedily as might be, and it was with a high heart that I strode along the sunset lanes, hearing for some time the chiming of her bell in front of me, till she had wheeled it quite out of hearing, and it was lost in the distance.

I never did a better five miles in my life.

CHAPTER III

TWO TOWN MICE AT A COUNTRY INN.

WHEN I reached the Wheel of Pleasure, I found Rosalind awaiting me in the coffee-room, looking fresh from a traveller's toilette, and with the welcome news that dinner was on the way. By the time I had washed off the day's dust it was ready, and a merry meal it proved. Rosalind had none of Alastor's objections to the wine-list, so we drank an excellent champagne; and as there seemed to be no one in the hotel but ourselves, we made ourselves at home and talked and laughed, none daring to make us afraid.

At first, on sitting down to table, we had grown momentarily shy, with one of those sudden freaks of self-consciousness which occasionally surprise one, when, midway in some slightly unconventional situation to which the innocence of nature has led us, we realise it — " for an instant and no more."

Positively, I think that in the embarrassment of that instant I had made some inspired
remark to Rosalind about the lovely country
which lay dreamy in the afterglow outside our
window.   Oh, yes, I remember the very
words.   They were " What a heavenly landscape ! " or something equally striking.

"Yes," Rosalind had answered, " it is
almost as beautiful as the Strand ! "

If I'd known her better, I should have
exclaimed, " You dear ! " and I think it pos
sible that I did say something to that effect, —
perhaps "You dear woman ! "   At all events,
the veil of self-consciousness was rent in
twain at that remark, and our spirits rushed
together at this touch of London nature thus
unexpectedly revealed.

London ! I had n't realised till this moment
how I had been missing it all these days of
rustication, and my heart went out to it with
a vast homesickness.

"Yes ! the Strand," I repeated tenderly,
" the Strand — at night ! "

" Indeed, yes ! what is more beautiful in
the whole world? " she joined in ardently.

" The wild torrents of light, the passionate

human music, the hansoms, the white shirts
and shawled heads, the theatres—"

"Don't speak of them or you'll make me
cry," said Rosalind.

"The little suppers after the theatre—"

"Please don't," she cried, "it is cruel;"
and I saw that her eyes were indeed glisten-
ing with tears.

"But, of course," I continued, to give a
slight turn aside in our talk, "it is very
wrong of us to have such sophisticated tastes.
We ought to love these lonely hills and
meadows far more. The natural man revels
in solitude, and wants no wittier company
than birds and flowers. Wordsworth made
a constant companion of a pet daisy. He
seldom went abroad without one or two trot-
ting at his side, and a skylark would keep
Shelley in society for a week."

"But they were poets," retorted Rosalind;
"you don't call poets natural. Why, they
are the most unnatural of men. The natural
person loves the society of his kind, whereas
the poet runs away from it."

"Well, of course, there are poets and
poets, poets sociable and poets very unso-

ciable. Wordsworth made the country, but
Lamb made the town; and there is quite a
band of poets nowadays who share his dis-
taste for mountains, and take London for
their muse. If you'll promise not to cry
again, I'll recall some lines by a friend of
mine which were written for town-tastes like
ours. But perhaps you know them?"

It will gratify my friend to learn that Rosalind had the verses I refer to by heart, and
started off humming, —

> "Ah, London, London, our delight,
> Great flower that opens but at night,
> Great city of the midnight sun,
> Whose day begins when day is done . . .
> Like dragon-flies the hansoms hover
> With jewelled eyes to catch the lover;"

and so on, with a gusto of appreciation that
must have been very gratifying to the author
had he been present.

Thus perceiving a taste for a certain modern style of poetry in my companion, I be-
thought me of a poem which I had written
on the roadside a few days before, and which,
I confess, I was eager to confide to some
sympathetic ear. I was diffident of quoting

it after such lines as Rosalind had recalled,
but by the time we had reached our coffee, I
plucked up courage to mention it. I had,
however, the less diffidence in that it would
have a technical interest for her, being indeed
no other than a song of cycling *à deux* which
had been suggested by one of those alarmist
danger-posts always placed at the top of the
pleasantest hills, sternly warning the cyclist
that "this hill is dangerous," — just as in life
there is always some minatory notice-board
frowning upon us in the direction we most
desire to take.

But I omit further preface and produce the
poem : —

> "This hill is dangerous," I said,
>   As we rode on together
> Through sunny miles and sunny miles
>   Of Surrey heather ;
> "This hill is dangerous — don't you think
>   We 'd better walk it?"
> "Or sit it out — more danger still !"
>   She smiled — "and talk it?"
>
> ' Are you afraid?" she turned and cried
>   So very brave and sweetly, —
> Oh that brave smile that takes the heart
>   Captive completely !

"Afraid?" I said, deep in her eyes
    Recklessly gazing;
"For you I 'd ride into the sun
    And die all blazing!"

"I never yet saw hill," I said,
    "And was afraid to take it;
I never saw a foolish law,
    And feared to break it.
Who fears a hill or fears a law
    With you beside him?
Who fears, dear star! the wildest sea
    With you to guide him?"

Then came the hill — a cataract,
    A dusty swirl, before us;
The world stood round — a village world —
    In fearful chorus.
Sure to be killed!   Sure to be killed!
    O fools, how dare ye!
Sure to be killed — and serve us right!
    Ah! love, but were we?

The hill was dangerous, we knew,
    And knew that we must take it;
The law was strong, — that too we knew,
    Yet dared to break it.
And those who 'd fain know how we fared
    Follow and find us,
Safe on the hills, with all the world
    Safely behind us.

Rosalind smiled as I finished. "I 'm afraid,"
she said, "the song is as dangerous as the

hill.   Of course it has more meanings than
one?"

"Perhaps two," I assented.

"And the second more important than
the first."

"Maybe," I smiled; "however, I hope
you like it."

Rosalind was very reassuring on that point,
and then said musingly, as if half to herself,
"But that hill is dangerous, you know;
and young people would do well to pay
attention to the danger-board!"

Her voice shook as she spoke the last two
or three words, and I looked at her in some
surprise.

"Yes, I know it," she added, her voice
quite broken; and before I realised what was
happening, there she was with her beautiful
head down upon the table, and sobbing as if
her heart would break.

"Forgive me for being such a fool," she
managed to wring out.

Now, usually I never interrupt a woman
when she is crying, as it only encourages her
to continue; but there was something so
unexpected and mysterious about Rosalind's

sudden outburst that it was impossible not to be sympathetic. I endeavoured to soothe her with such words as seemed fitting; and as she was crying because she really could n't help it, she did n't cry long.

These tears proved, what certain indications of manner had already hinted to me, that Rosalind was more artless than I had at first supposed. She was a woman of the world, in that she lived in it, and loved its gaieties, but there was still in her heart no little of the child, as is there not in the hearts of all good women — or men?

And this you will realise when I tell you the funny little story which she presently confided to me as the cause of her tears.

13

CHAPTER IV

MARRIAGE À LA MODE

FOR Rosalind was no victim of the monster
man, as you may have supposed her, no
illustration of his immemorial perfidies.
On the contrary, she was one half of a very
happy marriage, and, in a sense, her sufferings at the moment were merely theoretical,
if one may so describe the sufferings caused
by a theory.   But no doubt the reader would
prefer a little straightforward narrative.

Well, Rosalind and Orlando, as we may
as well call them, are two newly married
young people who 've been married, say, a
year, and who find themselves at the end of
it loving each other more than at the beginning, — for you are to suppose two of the
tenderest, most devoted hearts that ever
beat as one.   However, they are young
people of the introspective modern type,
with a new theory for everything.

About marriage and the law of happiness
in that blessed estate, they boasted the latest
philosophical patents.   To them, among
other matters, the secret of unhappy marriages was as simple as can be.   It was in
nothing more or less than the excessive "familiarity" of ordinary married life, and the
lack of personal freedom allowed both parties to the contract.   Thus love grew commonplace, and the unhappy ones to weary
of each other by excessive and enforced
association.   This was obvious enough, and
the remedy as obvious,—separate bedrooms,
and a month's holiday in each year to be
spent apart (notoriously all people of quality
had separate bedrooms, and see how happy
they were!).   These and similar other safe-
guards of individual liberty they had in
mock-earnest drawn up and signed on their
marriage eve, as a sort of supplemental
wedding service.

It would not be seemly to inquire how far
certain of these conditions had been kept, —
how often, for example, Orlando's little
hermit's bed had really needed remaking
during those twelve months!   Answer, ye

birds of the air that lie in your snug nests, so close, so close, through the tender summer nights, and maybe with two or three little ones besides, — unless, indeed, ye too have felt the influence of the Zeit-geist, and have taken to sleeping in separate nests.

The condition with which alone we have here to concern ourselves was one which provided that each of the two lovers, hereafter to be called the husband of the one part and the wife of the other part, solemnly bound themselves to spend one calendar month of each year out of each other's society, with full and free liberty to spend it wheresoever, with whomsoever, and howsoever they pleased; and that this condition was rigidly to be maintained, whatever immediate effort it might cost, as the parties thereto believed that so would their love the more likely maintain an enduring tenderness and an unwearied freshness. And to this did Orlando and his Rosalind set their hands and hearts and lips.

Now, wisdom is all very well till the time comes to apply it; and as that month of June approached in which they had designed

to give their love a holiday, they had found
their courage growing less and less.   Their
love did n't want a holiday; and when
Orlando had referred to the matter during
the early days of May, Rosalind had burst
into tears, and begged him to reconsider a
condition which they had made before they
really knew what wedded love was.   But
Orlando, though in tears himself (so Rosalind averred), had a higher sense of their
duty to their ideal, and was able, though in
tears, to beg her look beyond the moment,
and realise what a little self-denial now
might mean in the years to come.   They
had n't kept any other of their resolutions,
— thus Rosalind let it out! — this must be
kept.

And thus it had come about that Orlando
had gone off for his month's holiday with a
charming girl, who, with the cynic, will no
doubt account for his stern adherence to
duty; and Rosalind had gone off for hers
with a pretty young man whom she 'd liked
well enough to go to the theatre and to
supper with,—a young man who was indeed a
dear friend, and a vivacious, sympathetic

companion, but whom, as a substitute for
Orlando, she immediately began to hate.
Such is the female heart!

The upshot of the experiment, so far as
she was concerned, **was** that she had quar-
relled with her companion, and had gone off
in search of her husband, on which search
she was embarked at the moment of my en-
countering her. The tears, therefore, — that
is, the first lot of tears by the roadside, —
had not been all on account of the injured
bicycle, you see.

Now the question was, How had Orlando
been getting on? I had an intuition that in
his case the experiment had proved more
enjoyable, but I am not one to break the
bruised reed by making such a suggestion.
On the contrary, I expressed my firm conviction that Orlando was probably even more
miserable than she was.

"Do you really think so?" she asked
eagerly, her poor miserable face growing
bright a moment with hope and gratitude.

"Undoubtedly," I answered sententiously.
"To put the case on the most general principles, apart from Orlando's great love for

you, it is an eternal truth of masculine sentiment that man always longs for the absent woman."

"Are you quite sure?" asked Rosalind, with an unconvinced half-smile.

"Absolutely."

"I thought," she continued, "that it was just the other way about; that it was presence and not absence that made the heart of man grow fonder, and that if a man's best girl, so to say, was away, he was able to make himself very comfortable with his second-best!"

"In some cases, of course, it's true," I answered, unmoved; "but with a love like yours and Orlando's, it's quite different."

"Oh, do you really mean it?"

"Certainly I do; and your mistake has been in supposing that an experiment which no few every-day married couples would be only too glad to try, was ever meant for two such love-birds as you. Laws and systems are meant for the unhappy and the untractable, not for people like you, for whom Love makes its own laws."

"Yes, that is what we used to say; and

indeed, we thought that this was one of love's laws, — this experiment, as you call it."

"But it was quite a mistake," I went on in my character as matrimonial oracle. "Love never made a law so cruel, a law that would rob true lovers of each other's society for a whole month in a year, stretching them on the rack of absence — " There my period broke down, so I began another less ambitiously planned.

"A whole month in a year! Think what that would mean in a lifetime. How long do you expect to live and love together? Say another fifty years at the most. Well, fifty ones are fifty. Fifty months equal — four twelves are forty-eight and two over — four years and two months. Yes, out of the short life God allows even for the longest love you would voluntarily throw away four years and two months!"

This impressive calculation had a great effect on poor Rosalind; and it is a secondary matter that it and its accompanying wisdom may have less weight with the reader, as for the moment Rosalind was my one concern.

"But, of course, we have perfect trust in each other," said Rosalind presently, with charming illogicality.

"No doubt," I said; "but Love, like a good householder (ahem!), does well not to live too much on trust."

"But surely love means perfect trust," said Rosalind.

"Theoretically, yes; practically, no. On the contrary, it means exactly the opposite. Trust, perfect trust, with loved ones far away! No, it is an inhuman ideal, and the more one loves the less one lives up to it. If not, what do these tears mean?"

"Oh, no!" Rosalind retorted, with a flush, "you mustn't say that. I trust Orlando absolutely. It isn't that; it's simply that I can't bear to be away from him."

What women mean by "trusting" might afford a subject for an interesting disquisition. However, I forbore to pursue the matter, and answered Rosalind's remark in a practical spirit.

"Well, then," I said, "if that's all, the thing to do is to find Orlando, tell him that

you cannot bear it, and spend the rest of
your holiday, you and he, together."

"That's what I thought," said Rosalind.

"Unfortunately," I continued, "owing to
your foolish arrangement not to tell each
other where you were going and not to write,
as being incompatible with Perfect Trust,
you don't know where Orlando is at the
present moment."

"No; but I have a good guess," said
Rosalind. "There's a smart little watering-place, not so many miles from here,
called Yellowsands, a sort of secret little
Monaco, which not many people know of,
a wicked-innocent gay little place, where
we've often talked of going. I think it's
very likely that Orlando has gone there;
and that's just where I was going when we
met."

I will tell the reader more about Yellowsands in the next chapter. Meanwhile, let
us complete Rosalind's arrangements. The
result of our conversation was that she was
to proceed to Yellowsands on the morrow,
and that I was to follow as soon as possible,
so as to be available should she chance to

need any advice, and at all events to give myself the pleasure of meeting her again.

This arranged, we said good-night, Rosalind with ever such a brightened-up face, of which I thought for half an hour and then fell asleep to dream of Yellowsands.

CHAPTER V

CONCERNING THE HAVEN OF YELLOWSANDS

ON the morrow, at the peep of day, Rosalind was off to seek her lord. An hour or so after I started in leisurely pursuit.

Yellowsands! I had heard in a vague way of the place, as a whim of a certain young nobleman who combined brains with the pursuit of pleasure. Like most ideas, it was simple enough when once conceived. Any one possessing a mile or two of secluded seaboard, cut off on the land side by precipitous approaches, and including a sheltered river mouth ingeniously hidden by nature, in the form of a jutting wall of rock, from the sea, might have made as good use of these natural opportunities as the nobleman in question, had they only been as wise and as rich. William Blake proposed to rebuild Jerusalem in this green and pleasant

land. My lord proposed to erect a miniature Babylon amid similar pleasant surroundings, a little dream-city by the sea, a
home for the innocent pleasure-seeker stifled
by the puritanism of the great towns, *refu-
gium peccatorum* in this island of the saints.

"Once it was the Puritan Fathers who
left our coasts," he is recorded to have said;
"nowadays it is our Prodigal Sons."

No doubt it was in further elaboration of
this aphorism that the little steamboat that
sailed every other day from Yellowsands to
the beckoning shores of France was called
"the Mayflower."

My lord's plan had been simple. By the
aid of cunning architects he had first blasted
his harbour into shape, then built his hotels
and pleasure-palaces, and then leased them
to dependants of his who knew the right sort
of people, and who knew that it was as much
as their lease was worth to find accommodation for teetotal amateur photographers or
wistful wandering Sunday-school treats. As,
unfortunately, the Queen's highway ran
down in tortuous descent to the handful of
fishermen's cottages that had clung there

limpet-like for ages, there was always a chance of such a stray visitation; but it was remote, and the whole place, hand and heart, was in the pocket of my lord.

So much to give the reader some idea of the secret watering-place of Yellowsands, situated at the mouth of that romantic little torrent, the river Sly. Such further description as may be needed may be kept till we come within sight of its gilded roofs and marble terraces.

CHAPTER VI

THE MOORLAND OF THE APOCALYPSE

I RECKONED that it would take me two or three days, leisurely walking, to reach Yellowsands. Rosalind would, of course, arrive there long before me; but that I did not regret, as I was in a mood to find company in my own thoughts.

Her story gave me plenty to think of. I dwelt particularly on the careless extravagance of the happy. Here were two people to whom life had given casually what I was compelled to go seeking lonely and footsore through the world, and with little hope of finding it at the end; and yet were they so little aware of their good fortune as to risk it over a trumpery theory, a shadow of pseudo-philosophy. Out of the deep dark ocean of life Love had brought them his great moon-pearl, and they sat on the boat's edge carelessly tossing it from one to the other, unmindful of the hungry fathoms on every side. A sudden slip, and they had lost it for ever, and might only watch its shimmering fall to the bottom of the world. Theories! Theories are for the unknown and the unhappy. Who will trouble to theorise about Heaven when he has found Heaven itself? Theories are for the poor-devil outcast, — for him who stands outside the confectioner's shop of life without a penny in his pocket, while the radiant purchasers pass in and out through the doors, — for him who watches with wistful eyes this and that sugared marvel taken out of the window by mysterious hands, to bless some happy customer inside. He is not fool enough even to hope for one of those glistering masterpieces of frosted sugar and silk flowers, which rise to pinnacles of snowy sweetness, white mountains of blessedness, rich inside, they say, with untold treasures for the tooth that is sweet. No! he craves nothing but a simple Bath-bun of happiness, and even that is denied him.

Would I ever find my Bath-bun? I dis-

consolately asked myself.   I had been seeking it now for some little time, and seemed
no nearer than when I set out.   I had seen
a good many Bath-buns on my pilgrimage,
it is true.   Some I have not had space to
confide to the reader; but somehow or other
they had not seemed the unmistakably
predestined for which I was seeking.

And oh, how I could love a girl, if she
would only give me the chance, — that is,
be the right girl!   Oh, Sylvia Joy! where
art thou?   Why so long dost thou remain
hidden "in shady leaves of destiny"?

> "Seest thou thy lover lowly laid,
>   Hear'st thou the sighs that rend his breast?"

And then, as the novelists say, "a strange
thing happened."

The road I was tramping at the moment
was somewhat desolate.   It ran up from a
small market town through a dreary undulating moorland, forking off here and there
to unknown villages of which the horizon
gave no hint.   Its cheerless hillocks were
all but naked of vegetation, for a never very
flourishing growth of heather had recently

14

been burnt right down to the unkindly-
looking earth, leaving a dwarf black forest
of charred sticks very grim to the eye and
heart; while the dull surface of a small
lifeless-looking lake added the final touch to
the Dead-Sea mournfulness of the prospect.

Suddenly I became aware of the fluttering
of a grey dress a little ahead of me.   Uncon-
sciously I had been overtaking a tall young
woman walking in the same direction as myself, with a fine athletic carriage of her figure
and a noble movement of her limbs.

She walked manfully, and as I neared her
I could hear the sturdy ring of her well-shod
feet upon the road.   There was an air of
expectancy about her walk, as though she
looked to be met presently by some one due
from the opposite direction.

It was curious that I had not noticed her
before, for she must have been in sight
for some time.   No doubt my melancholy
abstraction accounted for that, and perhaps
her presence there was to be explained by a
London train which I had listlessly observed
come in to the town an hour before.   This
surmise was confirmed, as presently, over the

brow of a distant undulation in the road, I
descried a farmer's gig driven by another
young woman.   The gig immediately hoisted
a handkerchief; so did my pedestrian.   At
this moment I was within a yard or two of
overtaking her.   And it was then the strange
thing happened.

Distance had lent no enchantment which
nearness did not a hundred times repay.
The immediate impression of strength and
distinction which the first glimpse of her
had made upon me was more and more veri-
fied as I drew closer to her.   The carriage
of her head was no whit less noble than the
queenly carriage of her limbs, and her glorious chestnut hair, full of warm tints of
gold, was massed in a sumptuous simplicity
above a neck that would have made an
average woman's fortune.   This glowing
description, however, must be lowered or
heightened in tone by the association of
these characteristics with an undefinable
simplicity of mien, a certain slight rusticity
of effect.   The town spoke in her well-cut
gown and a few simple adornments, but the
dryad still moved inside.

I suppose most men, even in old age,
feel a certain anxiety, conscious or not, as
they overtake a woman whose back view
is in the least attractive.   I confess that I
felt a more than usual, indeed a quite irra-
tional, perturbation of the blood, as, coming level with her, I dared to look into her
face.   As I did so she involuntarily turned
to look at me — turned to look at me,
did I say?   "To look" is a feeble verb
indeed to express the unexpected shock of
beauty to which I was suddenly exposed.   I
cannot describe her features, for somehow
features always mean little to me.   They
were certainly beautifully moulded, and her
skin was of a lovely pale olive, but the life
of her face was in her great violet eyes and
her wonderful mouth.   Thus suddenly to
look into her face was like unexpectedly to
come upon moon and stars reflected in some
lonely pool.   I suppose the look lasted only a
second or two; but it left me dazzled as that
king in the Eastern tale, who seemed to have
lived whole dream-lives between dipping his
head into a bowl of water and taking it out
again.   Similarly in that moment I seemed

to have dived into this unknown girl's eyes, to have walked through the treasure palaces of her soul, to have stood before the flaming gates of her heart, to have gathered silver flowers in the fairy gardens of her dreams. I had followed her white-robed spirit across the moonlit meadows of her fancy, and by her side had climbed the dewy ladder of the morning star, and then suddenly I had been whirled up again to the daylight through the magic fountains of her eyes.

I 'll tell you more about that look presently! Meanwhile the gig approached, and the two girls exchanged affectionate greetings.

"Tom has n't come with you, then?" said the other girl, who was evidently her sister, and who was considerably more rustic in style and accent.   She said it with a curious mixture of anxiety and relief.

"No," answered the other simply, and I thought I noticed a slight darkening of her face.   Tom was evidently her husband.   So she was married!

"Yes!" said a fussy hypocrite of reason within me, "and what 's that to do with you?"

"Everything, you fool!" answered a ro-
buster voice in my soul, kicking the feeble
creature clean out of my head on the instant.

For, absurd as it may sound, with that
look into those Arabian Nights' eyes, had
come somewhere out of space an overwhelm-
ing intuition, nay, an unshakable conviction,
that the woman who was already being rolled
away from me down the road in that Dis's
car of a farmer's gig, was now and for ever
and before all worlds the woman God had
created for me, and that, unless I could be
hers and she mine, there would be no home,
no peace for either of us so long as we
lived.

And yet she was being carried away further
and further every moment, while I gazed
after her, aimlessly standing in the middle
of the road. Why did I not call to her,
overtake her?   In a few moments she would
be lost to me for ever —

Though I was unaware of it, this hesita-
tion was no doubt owing to a stealthy return
of reason by the back-door of my mind. In
fact, he presently dared to raise his voice
again. "I don't deny," he ventured, ready

any moment to flee for his life, "that she is written yours in all the stars, and particularly do I see it written on the face of the moon; but you must n't forget that many are thus meant for each other who never meet, not to speak of marrying.   It is such contradictions between the purposes and performance of the Creator that make life — life; you'll never see her again, so make your mind easy — "

At that moment the gig was on the point of turning a corner into a dark pine-wood; but just ere it disappeared, — was it fancy? — I seemed to have caught the flash of a momentarily fluttering handkerchief. "Won't I? you fool!" I exclaimed, savagely smiting reason on the cheek, as I sprang up wildly to wave mine; but the road was already blank.

At this a sort of panic possessed me, and like a boy I raced down the road after her. To lose her like this, at the very moment that she had been revealed to me.   It was more than I could bear. Past the dreary lake, through the little pine-wood I ran, and then I was brought to a halt, panting, by cross-roads and a finger-post. An involuntary memory of Nicolete sang to me as I read the quaint names of the villages to one of which the Vision was certainly wending. Yes! I was bound on one more journey to the moon, but alas! there was no heavenly being by my side to point the way. Oh, agony, which was the road she had taken?

It never occurred to me till the following day that I might have been able to track her by the wheel-marks of the gig on the dusty summer road. Instead I desperately resorted to the time-honoured expedient of setting up a stick and going in the direction of its fall. Like most ancient guide-posts, it led me quite wrong, down into a pig's-trough of a hamlet whither I felt sure she could n't have been bound. Then I ran back in a frenzy, and tried the other road, — as if it could be any use, with at least three quarters of an hour gone since I had lost sight of her. Of course I had no luck; and finally, hot and worn out with absurd excitement, I threw myself down in a meadow and called myself an ass, — which I undoubtedly was.

For of all the fancies that had obsessed

THE GOLDEN GIRL   217

my moonstruck brain, this was surely the
maddest.   Suppose I had overtaken the girl,
what could I have said to her?   And, suppose she had listened to me, how did I know
she was the girl I imagined her to be?
But this was sheer reason again, and has no
place in a fantastic romance.   So I hasten
to add that the mood was one of brief dura-
tion, and that no cold-water arguments were
able to quench the fire which those eyes had
set aflame within me, no daylight philosophy
had any power to dispel the dream of a face
which was now my most precious possession,
as I once more took up my stick and listlessly pursued my way to Yellowsands.

For I had one other reason than my own
infatuation, or thought I had.   Yes, brief
and rapid as our glance at each other had
been, I had fancied in her eyes a momentary
kindling as they met mine, a warm summer-
lightning which seemed for a second to light
up for me the inner heaven of her soul.

Of one feeling, however, I was sure, —
that on my side this apocalyptic recognition
of her, as it had seemed, was no mere passionate correspondence of sex, no mere spell

of a beautiful face (for such passion and such glamour I had made use of opportunities to study), but was indeed the flaming up of an elemental affinity, profounder than sex, deeper than reason, and ages older than speech.

But it was a fancy, for all that? Yes, one of those fancies that are fancies on earth, but facts in heaven. Perhaps you don't believe in them. Well, I 'm afraid that cannot be helped.

CHAPTER VII

"COME UNTO THESE YELLOW SANDS!"

NOTHING further happened to me till I
reached Yellowsands, except an exciting
ride on the mail-coach, which connected it
with the nearest railway-station some twenty
miles away. For the last three or four miles
the road ran along the extreme precipitous
verge of cliffs that sloped, a giant's wall of
grassy mountain, right away down to a dreamy
amethystine floor of sea, miles and miles, as
it seemed, below. To ride on that coach,
as it gallantly staggered betwixt earth and
heaven, was to know all the ecstasy of flying,
with an added touch of danger, which birds
and angels, and others accustomed to fly, can
never experience. And then at length the
glorious mad descent down three plunging
cataracts of rocky road, the exciting rattling
of the harness, the grinding of the strong
brakes, the driver's soothing calls to his

horses, and the long burnished horn trailing
wild music behind us, like invisible banners
of aerial brass, — oh, it stirred the dullest
blood amongst us thus as it were to tear
down the sky towards the white roofs of
Yellowsands, glittering here and there among
the clouds of trees which filled the little
valley almost to the sea's edge, while floating
up to us came soft strains of music, silken
and caressing, as though the sea itself sang
us a welcome.   Had you heard it from
aboard the Argo, you would have declared
it to be the sirens singing, and it would have
been found necessary to lash you to the
mast.   But there were no masts to lash you
to in Yellowsands — and of the sirens it is
not yet time to speak.

It was the golden end of afternoon as the
coach stopped in front of the main hotel,
The Golden Fortune; and for the benefit of
any with not too long purses who shall hereafter light on Yellowsands, and be alarmed
at the name and the marble magnificence of
that delightful hotel, I may say that the
charges there were surprisingly " reasonable," owing to one other wise provision of

the young lord and master of that happy
place, who had had the wit to realise that
the nicest and brightest and prettiest people
were often the poorest. Yellowsands, therefore, was carried on much like a club, to
which you had only to be the right sort of
person to belong. I was relieved to find
that the hotel people evidently considered
me the right sort of person, and did n't
take me for a Sunday-school treat, — for
presently I found myself in a charming little
corner bedroom, whence I could survey the
whole extent of the little colony of pleasure.
The Golden Fortune was curiously situated, perched at the extreme sea-end of a
little horse-shoe bay hollowed out between
two headlands, the points of which approached each other so closely that the
river Sly had but a few yards of rocky channel through which to pour itself into the sea.
The Golden Fortune, therefore, backed by
towering woodlands, looked out to sea at
one side, across to the breakwater headland
on another, and on its land side commanded
a complete view of the gay little haven, with
its white houses built terrace on terrace upon

its wooded slopes, connected by flights of zigzag steps, by which the apparently inaccessible shelves and platforms circulated their gay life down to the gay heart of the place, — the circular boulevard, exquisitely leafy and cool, where one found the great casino and the open-air theatre, the exquisite orchestra, into which only the mellowest brass and the subtlest strings were admitted, and the Café du Ciel, charmingly situated among the trees, where the boulevard became a bridge, for a moment, at the mouth of the river Sly. Here one might gaze up the green rocky defile through which the Sly made pebbly music, and through which wound romantic walks and natural galleries, where far inland you might wander

> " From dewy dawn to dewy night,
> And have one with you wandering,"

or where you might turn and look across the still lapping harbour, out through the little neck of light between the headlands to the shimmering sea beyond, — your ears filled with a melting tide of sweet sounds, the murmur of the streams and the gentle surging of the sea, the rippling of leaves, the soft restless whisper of women's gowns, and the music of their vowelled voices. It was here I found myself sitting at sunset, alone, but so completely under the spell of the place that I needed no companion. The place itself was companion enough. The electric fairy lamps had popped alight; and as the sun sank lower, Yellowsands seemed like a glowing crown of light floating upon the water.

I had as yet failed to catch any sight of Rosalind; so I sat alone, and so far as I had any thoughts or feelings, beyond a consciousness of heavenly harmony with my surroundings, they were for that haunting unknown face with the violet eyes and the heavy chestnut hair.

Presently, close by, the notes of a guitar came like little gold butterflies out of the twilight, and then a woman's voice rose like a silver bird on the air. It was a gay wooing measure to which she sang. I listened with ears and heart. " All ye," it went, —

> All ye who seek for pleasure,
> Here find it without measure —

No one to say
A body nay,
And naught but love and leisure.

All ye who seek forgetting,
Leave frowns and fears and fretting,
Here by the sea
Are fair and free
To give you peace and petting.

All ye whose hearts are breaking
For somebody forsaking,
We 'll count you dear,
And heal you here,
And send you home love-making.

" Bravo ! " I cried involuntarily, as the
song ended amid multitudinous applause ;
and I thus attracted the attention of another
who sat near me as lonely as myself, but
evidently quite at home in the place.

" You have n't heard our sirens sing
before? " he said, turning to me with a
pleasant smile, and thus we fell into talk of
the place and its pleasures.

" There 's one feature of the place I might
introduce you to if you care for a stroll,"
he said presently. " Have you heard of
The Twelve Golden-Haired Bar-maids ? " I
had n't, but the fantastic name struck my

fancy.   It was, he explained, the name given to a favourite buffet at the Hotel Aphrodite, which was served by twelve wonderful girls, not one under six feet in height, and all with the most glorious golden hair.   It was a whim of the management, he said.

So, of course, we went.

15

CHAPTER VIII

THE TWELVE GOLDEN-HAIRED BAR-MAIDS.

NOW it was not without some boyish nervousness that I followed my newly made friend, for I confess that I have ever been a poor hand at talking to bar-maids. It is, I am convinced, an art apart, an art like any other, — needing first the natural gift, then the long patient training, and finally the courageous practice. Alas for me, I possessed neither gift, training, nor courage. Courage I lacked most of all. It was in vain that I said to myself that it was like swimming, — all that was needed was " confidence." That was the very thing I could n't muster. No doubt I am handicapped by a certain respectful homage which I always feel involuntarily to any one in the shape of woman, for anything savouring of respect is the last thing to win the bar-maid heart divine. The man to win her is he who calls loudly for his drink, without a " Please " or a " Thank you," throws his hat at the back of his head, gulps down half his glass, and, while drawing breath for the other half, takes a hard, indifferent look at her, and in an off-hand voice throws her some fatuous, mirthless jest.

Now, I've never been able to do this in the convincing grand manner of the British male; and whatever I have said, the effect has been the same. I've talked about theatres and music-halls, of events of the day, I've even — Heaven help me — talked of racing and football, but I might as well have talked of Herbert Spencer. I suppose I did n't talk about them in the right way. I'm sure it must be my fault somewhere, for certainly they seem easy enough to please, poor things ! However, my failure remains, and sometimes even I, find it extremely hard to attract their attention in the ordinary way of business. I don't mind my neighbour being preferred before me, but I do object to his being served before me !

So, I say, I could n't but tremble at the vision of those golden-haired goddesses, standing with immobile faces by their awful altars.

Indeed, had I realised how superbly impressive they were going to be, I think I must have declined the adventure altogether, — for, robed in lustrous ivory-white linen were those figures of undress marble, the wealth of their glorious bodies pressing out into bosoms magnificent as magnolias (nobler lines and curves Greece herself has never known), towering in throats of fluted alabaster, and flowering in coiffures of imperial gold. Nor was their temple less magnificent. To make it fair, Ruskin had relit the seven lamps of architecture, and written the seven labours of Hercules; for these windows through a whole youth Burne Jones had worshipped painted glass at Oxford, and to breathe romance into these frescos had Rossetti been born, and Dante born again. Men had gone to prison and to death that this temple of Whiskey-and-Soda might be fair.

Strange, in truth, are the ministrations to which Beauty is called. Out of the high heaven is she summoned, from mystic communion with her own perfection, from majestic labours in the Sistine Chapel of the Stars, — yea, she must put aside her gold-leaf and purples and leave unfinished the very panels of the throne of God, — that Circe shall have her palace, and her worshippers their gilded sty.

As there were at least a score of "worshippers" round each Circe, my nervousness became unimportant, and therefore passed. Thus, as my companion and I sat at one of the little tables, from which we might gaze upon the sea without and Aphrodite within, my eyes were able to fly like bees from one fair face to another. Finally, they settled upon a Circe less besieged of the hoarse and grunting mob. She was conspicuously less in height, her hair was rather bright red than golden, and her face had more meanings than the faces of her fellows.

"Why," in a flash it came to me, "it's Rosalind!" and clean forgetting to be shy, or polite to my companion, I hastened across to her, to be greeted instantly in a manner so exclusively intimate that the little crowd about her presently spread itself among the other crowds, and we were left to talk alone.

"Well," I said, "you're a nice girl! Whatever are you doing here?"

"Yes, I'm afraid you'll have but a strange opinion of me," she said; "but I love all experience, — it's such fun, — and when I heard that there was a sudden vacancy for a golden-haired beauty in this place, I couldn't resist applying, and to my surprise they took me — and here I am! Of course I shall only stay till Orlando appears — which," she added mournfully — "he hasn't done yet."

Her hours were long and late, but she had two half-days free in the week, and for these of course I engaged myself.

Meanwhile I spent as much time as I decently could at her side; but it was impossible to monopolise her, and the rest of my time there was no difficulty in filling up, you may be sure, in so gay a place.

Two or three nights after this, a little before dinner-time, while I was standing talking to her, she suddenly went very white, and in a fluttering voice gasped, "Look yonder!" I looked. A rather slight dark-haired young man was entering the bar, with a very stylish pretty woman at his side. As they sat down and claimed the waiter, some

distance away, Rosalind whispered, "That's
my husband!"

"Oh!" I said; "but that's no reason for
your fainting. Pull yourself together. Take
a drop of brandy." But woman will never
take the most obvious restorative, and Rosalind presently recovered without the brandy.
She looked covertly at her husband, with
tragic eyes.

"He's much younger than I imagined
him," I said, — reserving for myself the satisfaction which this discovery had for me.

"Oh, yes, he's really quite a boy," said
Rosalind; adding under her breath, "Dear
fellow! how I love him!"

"And hate him too!" she superadded, as
she observed his evident satisfaction with his
present lot. Indeed the experiment appeared
to be working most successfully with him;
nor, looking at his companion, could I wonder. She was a sprightly young woman,
very smart and merry and decorously voluptuous, and of that fascinating prettiness that
wins the hearts of boys and storms the footlights. One of her characteristics soothed
the heart of Rosalind. She had splendid red
hair, almost as good as her own.

"He's been faithful to my hair, at all events," she said, trying to be nonchalant.

"And the eyes are not unlike," I added, meaning well.

"I'm sorry you think so," said Rosalind, evidently piqued.

"Well, never mind," I tried to make peace, "she hasn't your hands," — I knew that women cared more about their hands than their faces.

"How do you know?" she retorted; "you cannot see through her gloves."

"Would any gloves disguise your hands?" I persisted. "They would shine through the mittens of an Esquimau."

"Well, enough of that! See — I know it's wickedly mean of me — but couldn't you manage to sit somewhere near them and hear what they are saying? Of course you needn't tell me anything it would be mean to hear, but only what — "

"You would like to know."

But this little plot died at its birth, for that very minute the threatened couple arose, and went out arm in arm, apparently as absurdly happy as two young people can be.

As they passed out, one of Rosalind's
fellow bar-maids turned to her and said, —

" You know who that was? "

"Who ? " said Rosalind, startled.

" That pretty woman who went out with
that young Johnny just now ? "

" No ;. who is she ? "

" Why, that's " — and readers with heart-
disease had better brace themselves up for a
great shock — " that's

SYLVIA JOY,

the famous dancer! "

CHAPTER IX

SYLVIA JOY

SYLVIA JOY! And I hadn't so much as looked at her petticoat for weeks! But I would now. The violet eyes and the heavy chestnut hair rose up in moralising vision. Yes! God knows, they were safe in my heart, but petticoats were another matter. Sylvia Joy! Well, did you ever? Well, I'm d——d! Sylvia Joy!

I should have been merely superhuman had I been able to control the expression of surprise which convulsed my countenance at the sound of that most significant name.

"The name seems familiar to you," said Rosalind, a little surprised and a little eagerly; "do you know the lady?"

"Slightly," I prevaricated.

"How fortunate!" exclaimed Rosalind; "you'll be all the better able to help me!"

"Yes," I said; "but since things have turned out so oddly, I may say that our relations are of so extremely delicate a nature that I shall have very carefully to think out what is best to be done. Meanwhile, do you mind lending me that ring for a few hours?"

It was a large oblong opal set round with small diamonds, — a ring of distinguished design you could hardly help noticing, especially on a man's hand, for which it was too conspicuously dainty. I slipped it on the little finger of my left hand, and, begging Rosalind to remain where she was meanwhile, and to take no steps without consulting me, I mysteriously, not to say officiously, departed.

I left the twelfth Golden-Haired Bar-maid not too late to stalk her husband and her under-study to their hotel, where they evidently proposed to dine. There was, therefore, nothing left for me but to dine also. So I dined; and when the courses of my dining were ended, I found myself in a mellow twilight at the Café du Ciel. And it was about the hour of the sirens' singing.

Presently the little golden butterflies flitted once more through the twilight, and again the woman's voice rose like a silver bird on the air.

As I have a partiality for her songs, I transcribe this *Hymn of the Daughters of Aphrodite*, which you must try to imagine transfigured by her voice and the sunset.

Queen Aphrodite's
    Daughters are we,
She that was born
Of the morn
    And the sea;
White are our limbs
    As the foam on the wave,
Wild are our hymns
    And our lovers are brave !

Queen Aphrodite,
Born of the sea,
Beautiful dutiful daughters
Are we !

You who would follow,
    Fear not to come,
For love is for love
As dove is for dove ;
The harp of Apollo
    Shall lull you to rest,
And your head find its home
    On this beautiful breast.

Queen Aphrodite,
Born of the sea,
Beautiful dutiful daughters
Are we!

Born of the Ocean,
    Wave-like are we!
Rising and falling
    Like waves of the sea;
Changing for ever,
    Yet ever the same,
Music in motion
    And marble in flame.

Queen Aphrodite,
Born of the sea,
Beautiful dutiful daughters
Are we!

When I alighted once more upon the earth
from the heaven of this song, who should I
find seated within a table of me but the very
couple I was at the moment so unexpectedly
interested in? But they were far too absorbed
in each other to notice me, and consequently
I was able to hear all of importance that was
said. I regret that I cannot gratify the
reader with a report of their conversation,
for the excuse I had for listening was one
that is not transferable. A woman's happiness was at stake. No other consideration

could have persuaded me to means so mean save an end so noble. I did n't even tell Rosalind all I heard. Mercifully for her, the candour of fools is not among my superstitions. Suffice it for all third persons to know — what Rosalind indeed has never known, and what I hope no reader will be fool enough to tell her — that Orlando was for the moment hopelessly and besottedly faithless to his wife, and that my services had been bespoken in the very narrowest nick of time.

Having, as the reader has long known, a warm personal interest in his attractive companion, and desiring, therefore, to think as well of her as possible, I was pleased to deduce, negatively, from their conversation, that Sylvia Joy knew nothing of Rosalind, and believed Orlando to be a free, that is, an unmarried man. From the point of view, therefore, of her code, there was no earthly reason why she should not fall in with Orlando's proposal that they should leave for Paris by the "Mayflower" on the following morning. Orlando, I could hear, wished to make more extended arrangements,

and references to that well-known rendez-
vous, "Eternity," fell on my ears from time
to time. Evidently Sylvia had no very
saving belief in Eternity, for I heard her
say that they might see how they got on in
Paris for a start.   Then it would be time
enough to talk of Eternity.   This and other
remarks of Sylvia's considerably predisposed
me towards her.   Having concluded their
arrangements for the heaven of the morrow,
they rose to take a stroll along the boule-
vards. As they did so, I touched Orlando's
shoulder and begged his attention for a moment.   Though an entire stranger to him, I
had, I said, a matter of extreme importance
to communicate to him, and I hoped, there
fore, that it would suit his convenience to
meet me at the same place in an hour and a
half. As I said this, I flashed his wife's ring
in the light so obviously that he was compelled to notice it.

"Wherever did you get that?" he gasped,
no little surprised and agitated.

"From your wife," I answered, rapidly
moving away. "Be sure to be here at
eleven."

I slipped away into the crowd, and spent my hour and a half in persuading Rosalind that her husband was no doubt a little infatuated, but nevertheless the most faithful husband in the world. If she would only leave all to me, by this time to-morrow night, if not a good many hours before, he should be in her arms as safe as in the Bank. It did my heart good to see how happy this artistic adaptation of the truth made her; and I must say that she never had a wiser friend.

When eleven came, I was back in my seat at the Café du Ciel. Orlando too was excitedly punctual.

"Well, what is it?" he hurried out, almost before he had sat down.

"What will you do me the honour of drinking?" I asked calmly.

"Oh, drink be d——d!" he said; "what have you to tell me?"

"I 'm glad to hear you rap out such a good honest oath," I said; "but I should like a drink, for all that, and if I may say so, you would be none the worse for a brandy and soda, late as it is."

When the drinks had come, I remarked to
him quietly, but not without significance:
"The meaning of this ring is that your wife
is here, and very wretched.   By an accident
I have been privileged with her friendship;
and I may say, to save time, that she has
told me the whole story.

"What happily she has not been able to
tell me, and what I need hardly say she will
never know from me, I overheard, in the
interests of your joint happiness, an hour or
so ago."

The man who is telling the story has a
proverbial great advantage; but I hope the
reader knows enough of me by this to believe
that I am far from meanly availing myself
of it in this narrative.   I am well and grate-
fully aware that in this interview with
Orlando my advantages were many and
fortunate.   For example, had he been bigger
and older, or had he not been a gentleman,
my task had been considerably more arduous,
not to say dangerous.

But, as Rosalind had said, he was really
quite a boy, and I confess I was a little
ashamed for him, and a little piqued, that

16

he showed so little fight. The unexpected-
ness of my attack had, I realised, given me
the whip-hand. So I judged, at all events,
from the fact that he forbore to bluster, and
sat quite still, with his head in his hands, saying never a word for what seemed several minutes. Then presently he said very quietly, —

"I love my wife all the same."

"Of course you do," I answered, eagerly
welcoming the significant announcement;
"and if you'll allow me to say so, I think I
understand more about the whole situation
than either of you, bachelor though unfortunately I am. As a famous friend of mine is
fond of saying, lookers-on see most of the
game."

Then I rapidly told him the history of my
meeting with his wife, and depicted, in har-
rowing pigments of phrase, the distress of
her mind.

"I love my wife all the same," he repeated,
as I finished; "and," he added, "I love
Sylvia too."

"But not quite in the same way?" I
suggested.

"I love Sylvia very tenderly," he said.

"Yes, I know; I don't think you could do anything else.   No man worth his salt could be anything but tender to a dainty little woman like that.   But tenderness, gentleness, affection, even self-sacrifice, — these may be parts of love; but they are merely the crude untransformed ingredients of a love such as you feel for your wife, and such as I know she feels for you."

"She still loves me, then," he said pitifully; "she has n't fallen in love with you."

"No fear," I answered; "no such luck for me.   If she had, I 'm afraid I should hardly have been talking to you as I am at this moment.   If a woman like Rosalind, as I call her, gave me her love, it would take more than a husband to rob me of it, I can tell you."

"Yes," he repeated, "on my soul, I love her.   I have never been false to her, in my heart; but — "

"I know all about it," I said; "may I tell you how it all was, — diagnose the situation?"

"Do," he replied; "it is a relief to hear you talk."

"Well," I said, "may I ask one rather intimate question? Did you ever before you were married sow what are known as wild oats?"

"Never," he answered indignantly, flashing for a moment.

"Well, you should have done," I said; "that's just the whole trouble. Wild oats will get sown some time, and one of the arts of life is to sow them at the right time, — the younger the better. Think candidly before you answer me."

"I believe you are right," he replied, after a long pause.

"You are a believer in theories," I continued, "and so am I; but you can take my word that on these matters not all, but some, of the old theories are best. One of them is that the man who does not sow his wild oats before marriage will sow them afterwards, with a whirlwind for the reaping."

Orlando looked up at me, haggard with confession.

"You know the old story of the ring given to Venus? Well, it is the ruin of no few men to meet Venus for the first time on their marriage night. Their very chastity, paradoxical as it may seem, is their destruction. No one can appreciate the peace, the holy satisfaction of monogamy till he has passed through the wasting distractions, the unrest of polygamy. Plunged right away into monogamy, man, unexperienced in his good fortune, hankers after polygamy, as the monotheistic Jew hankered after polytheism; and thus the monogamic young man too often meets Aphrodite for the first time, and makes future appointments with her, in the arms of his pure young wife. If you have read Swedenborg, you will remember his denunciation of the lust of variety. Now, that is a lust every young man feels, but it is one to be satisfied before marriage. Sylvia Joy has been such a variant for you; and I'm afraid you're going to have some little trouble to get her off your nerves. Tell me frankly," I said, "have you had your fill of Aphrodite? It is no use your going back to your wife till you have had that."

"I'm not quite a beast," he retorted. "After all, it was an experiment we both agreed to try."

"Certainly," I answered, "and I hope it may have the result of persuading you of the unwisdom of experimenting with happiness. You have the realities of happiness; why should you trouble about its theories? They are for unhappy people, like me, who must learn to distil by learned patience the *aurum potabile* from the husks of life, the peace which happier mortals find lying like manna each morn upon the meadows."

"Well," I continued, "enough of the abstract; let us have another drink, and tell me what you propose to do."

"Poor Sylvia!" sighed Orlando.

"Shall I tell you about Sylvia?" I said. "On second thoughts, I won't. It would hardly be fair play; but this, I may say, relying on your honour, that if you were to come to my hotel, I could show you indisputable proof that I know at least as much about Sylvia Joy as even such a privileged intimate as yourself."

"It is strange, then, that she never recognised you just now," he retorted, with forlorn alertness.

"Of course she did n't. How young you

are! It is rather too bad of a woman of Sylvia's experience."

"And I've bought our passages for to-morrow. I cannot let her go without some sort of good-bye."

"Give the tickets to me. I can make use of them. How much are they? Let's see."

The calculation made and the money passed across, I said abruptly, —

"Now supposing we go and see your wife."

"You have saved my life," he said hoarsely, pressing my hand as we rose.

"I don't know about that," I said inwardly; "but I do hope I have saved your wife."

As I thought of that, a fear occurred to me.

"Look here," I said, as we strolled towards the Twelve Golden-Haired, "I hope you have no silly notions about confession, about telling the literal truth and so on. Because I want you to promise me that you will lie stoutly to your wife about Sylvia Joy. You must swear the whole thing has been platonic. It's the only chance for your happiness. Your wife, no doubt, will lure you on to confession by saying that she does n't mind this, that, and the other, so long as you don't keep it from her; and no doubt she will mean it till you have confessed. But, however good their theories, women by nature cannot help confusing body and soul, and what to a man is a mere fancy of the senses, to them is a spiritual tragedy. Promise me to lie stoutly on this point. It is, I repeat, the only chance for your future happiness. As has been wisely said, a lie in time saves nine; and such a lie as I advise is but one of the higher forms of truth. Such lying, indeed, is the art of telling the truth. The truth is that you love her body, soul, and spirit; any accidental matter which should tend to make her doubt that would be the only real lie. Promise me, won't you?"

"Yes, I will lie," said Orlando.

"Well, there she is," I said; "and God bless you both."

CHAPTER X

IN WHICH ONCE MORE I BECOME OCCUPIED IN MY OWN AFFAIRS

DURING a pause in my matrimonial lecture, Orlando had written a little farewell note to Sylvia, — a note which, of course, I did n't read, but which it is easy to imagine "wild with all regret." This I undertook to have delivered to her the same night, and promised to call upon her on the morrow, further to illuminate the situation, and to offer her every consolation in my power. To conclude the history of Orlando and his Rosalind, I may say that I saw them off from Yellowsands by the early morning coach. There was a soft brightness in their faces, as though rain had fallen in the night; but it was the warm sweet rain of joy that brings the flowers, and is but sister to the sun. They are, at the time of my writing, quite

old friends of mine, and both have an exces·
sive opinion of my wisdom and good-nature.

"That lie," Orlando once said to me long
after, "was the truest thing I ever said in
my life,"—a remark which may not give the
reader a very exalted idea of his general
veracity.

As the coach left long before pretty young
actresses even dreamed of getting up, I had
to control my impatient desire to call on
Mademoiselle Sylvia Joy till it was fully
noon.   And even then she was not to be
seen.   I tried again in the afternoon with
better success.

Rain had been falling in the night with
her too, I surmised, but it had failed to dim
her gay eyes, and had left her complexion
unimpaired.   Of course her little affair with
Orlando had never been very serious on her
side.   She genuinely liked him.   "He was
a nice kind boy," was the height of her passionate expression, and she was, naturally, a
little disappointed at having an affectionate
companion thus unexpectedly whisked off
into space.   Her only approach to anger was
on the subject of his deceiving her about

his wife. Little Sylvia Joy had no very
long string of principles; but one generous
principle she did hold by, — never, if she
knew it, to rob another woman of her husband. And that did make her cross with
Orlando. He had not played the game fair.

There is no need to follow, step by step,
the progression by which Sylvia Joy and I,
though such new acquaintances, became in
the course of a day or two even more intimate than many old friends. We took to
each other instinctively, even on our first
rather difficult interview, and very gently
and imperceptibly I bid for the vacant place
in her heart.

That night we dined together.

The next day we lunched and dined
together.

The next day we breakfasted, lunched,
and dined together.

And on the next I determined to venture
on the confession which, as you may imagine,
it had needed no little artistic control not to
make on our first meeting.

She looked particularly charming this
evening, in a black silk gown, exceedingly

simple and distinguished in style, throwing
up the lovely firm whiteness of her throat
and bosom, and making a fine contrast with
her lurid hair.

It was sheer delight to sit opposite her
at dinner, and quietly watch her without a
word. Shall I confess that I had an exceedingly boyish vanity in thus being granted
her friendship? It is almost too boyish to
confess at my time of life. It was simply in
the fact that she was an actress, — a real,
live, famous actress, whose photographs
made shop windows beautiful, — come right
out of my boy's fairyland of the theatre,
actually to sit eating and drinking, quite in
a real way, at my side. This, no doubt,
will seem pathetically naïve to most modern young men, who in this respect begin
where I leave off. An actress! Great
heavens! an actress is the first step to a
knowledge of life. Besides, actresses off the
stage are either brainless or soulful, and the
choice of evils is a delicate one. Well, I
have never set up for a man of the world,
though sometimes when I have heard the
Lovelaces of the day hinting mysteriously at

their secret sins or boasting of their florid gallantries, I have remembered the last verse of Suckling's "Ballad of a Wedding," which, no doubt, the reader knows as well as I, and if not, it will increase his acquaintance with our brave old poetry to look it up.

"You are very beautiful to-night," I said, in one of the meditative pauses between the courses.

"Thank you, kind sir," she said, making a mock courtesy; "but the compliment is made a little anxious for me by your evident implication that I did n't look so beautiful this morning.   You laid such a marked emphasis on to-night."

"Nay," I returned, "'for day and night are both alike to thee.'   I think you would even be beautiful — well, I cannot imagine any moment or station of life you would not beautify."

"I must get you to write that down, and then I'll have it framed.   It would cheer me of a morning when I curl my hair," laughed Sylvia.

"But you are beautiful," I continued, becoming quite impassioned.

"Yes, and as good as I'm beautiful."

And she was too, though perhaps the beauty occasionally predominated.

When the serious business of dining was dispatched, and we were trifling with our coffee and liqueurs, my eyes, which of course had seldom left her during the whole meal, once more enfolded her little ivory and black silk body with an embrace as real as though they had been straining passionate arms; and as I thus nursed her in my eyes, I smiled involuntarily at a thought which not unnaturally occurred to me.

"What is that sly smile about?" she asked. Now I had smiled to think that underneath that stately silk, around that tight little waist, was a dainty waistband bearing the legend "Sylvia Joy," No. 4, perhaps, or 5, but *not* No. 6; and a whole wonderful underworld of lace and linen and silk stockings, the counterpart of which wonders, my clairvoyant fancy laughed to think, were at the moment — so entirely unsuspected of their original owner — my delicious possessions.

Everything a woman wears or touches

immediately incarnates something of herself.   A handkerchief, a glove, a flower, —
with a breath she endues them with immortal
souls.   How much, therefore, of herself
must inhere in a garment so confidential as
a petticoat, or so close and constant a companion as a stocking!

Now that I knew Sylvia Joy, I realised
how absolutely true my instinct had been,
when on that far afternoon in that Surrey
garden I had said, "With such a petticoat
and such a name, Sylvia herself cannot be
otherwise than charming."

Indeed, now I could see that the petticoat
was nothing short of a portrait of her, and
that any one learned in the physiognomy of
clothes would have been able to pick Sylvia
out of a thousand by that spirited, spoilt,
and petted garment.

"What is that sly smile about?" she
repeated presently.

"I only chanced to think of an absurd
little fairy story I read the other day," I
said, "which is quite irrelevant at the moment.   You know the idle way things come
and go through one's head."

"I don't believe you," she replied, "but tell me the story. I love fairy tales."

"Certainly," I said, for I was n't likely to get a better opportunity. "There 's nothing much in it; it 's merely a variation of Cinderella's slipper. Well, once upon a time there was an eccentric young prince who 'd had his fling in his day, but had arrived at the lonely age of thirty without having met a woman whom he could love enough to make his wife. He was a rather fanciful young prince, accustomed to follow his whims; and one day, being more than usually bored with existence, he took it into his head to ramble incognito through his kingdom in search of his ideal wife, — 'The Golden Girl,' as he called her. He had hardly set out when in a country lane he came across a peasant girl hanging out clothes to dry, and he fell to talk with her while she went on with her charming occupation. Presently he observed, pegged on the line, strangely incongruous among the other homespun garments, a wonderful petticoat, so exquisite in material and design that it aroused his curiosity. At the same moment he noticed a pair of stockings,

round the tops of which one of the daintiest
artists in the land had wrought an exquisite
little frieze. The prince was learned in
every form of art, and had not failed to study
this among other forms of decoration. No
sooner did he see this petticoat than the
whim seized him that he would find and
marry the wearer, whoever she might
be — "

"Rather rash of him," interrupted Sylvia,
"for it is usually old ladies who have the
prettiest petticoats. They can best afford
them — "

"He questioned the girl as to their
owner," I continued, "and after vainly
pretending that they were her own, she
confessed that they had belonged to a young
and beautiful lady who had once lodged there
and left them behind. Then the prince gave
her a purse of gold in exchange for the
finery, and on the waistband of the petticoat
he read a beautiful name, and he said, ' This
and no other shall be my wife, this unknown
beautiful woman, and on our marriage night
she shall wear this petticoat.' And then the
prince went forth seeking — "

"There's not much point in it," interrupted Sylvia.

"No," I said, "I'm afraid I've stupidly
missed the point."

"Why, what was it?"

"The name upon the petticoat!"

"Why, what name was it?" she asked,
somewhat mystified.

"The inscription upon the petticoat was,
to be quite accurate, ' Sylvia Joy, No. 6.'"

"Whatever are you talking about?" she
said with quite a stormy blush. "I'm
afraid you've had more than your share of
the champagne."

As I finished, I slipped out of my pocket
a dainty little parcel softly folded in white
tissue paper. Very softly I placed it on the
table. It contained one of the precious
stockings; and half opening it, I revealed to
Sylvia's astonished eyes the cunning little
frieze of Bacchus and Ariadne, followed by
a troop of Satyrs and Bacchantes, which the
artist had designed to encircle one of the
white columns of that little marble temple
which sat before me.

"You know," I said, "how in fairy tales,

when the wandering hero or the maiden in distress has a guiding dream, the dream often leaves something behind on the pillow to assure them of its authenticity. ' When you wake up,' the dream will say, ' you will find a rose or an oak-leaf or an eagle's feather, or whatever it may be, on your pillow.' Well, I have brought this stocking — for which, if I might but use them, I have at the moment a stock of the most appropriately endearing adjectives — for the same purpose. By this token you will know that the fairy tale I have been telling you is true, and to-morrow, if you will, you shall see your autograph petticoat."

"Why, wherever did you come across them? And what a mad creature you must be! and what an odd thing that you should really meet me, after all!" exclaimed Sylvia, all in a breath. "Of course, I remember," she said frankly, and with a shade of sadness passing over her face. "I was spending a holiday with Jack Wentworth, — why, it must be nearly two years ago. Poor Jack! he was killed in the Soudan," and poor Jack could have wished no prettier resurrection than the look of tender memory that came into her face as she spoke of him, and the soft baby tears filled her eyes.

"I'm so sorry," I said. "Of course I did n't know. Let's come for a little stroll. There seems to be a lovely moon."

"Of course you did n't, she said, patting my cheek with a kind little hand. "Yes, do let us go for a stroll."

CHAPTER XI

"THE HOUR FOR WHICH THE YEARS DID SIGH"

THIS unexpected awakening of an old tenderness naturally prevented my speaking any more of my mind to Sylvia that evening. No doubt the reader may be a little astonished to hear that I had decided to offer her marriage, — not taking my serious view of a fanciful vow. Doubtless Sylvia was not entirely suitable to me, and to marry her was to be faithless to that vision of the highest, that wonderful unknown woman of the apocalyptic moorland, whose face Sylvia had not even momentarily banished from my dreams, and whom, with an unaccountable certitude, I still believed to be the woman God had destined for me; but, all things considered, Sylvia was surely as pretty an

answer to prayer as a man could reasonably
hope for.   Many historic vows had met with
sadly less lucky fulfilment.

So, after dinner the following evening, I
suggested that we should for once take a
little walk up along the river-side ; and when
we were quiet in the moonlight, dappling
the lovers' path we were treading, and making sharp contrasts of ink and silver down
in the river-bed, — I spoke.

" Sylvia," I said, plagiarising a dream which
will be found in Chapter IV., — " Sylvia, I
have sought you through the world and
found you at last; and with your gracious
permission, having found you, I mean to stick
    you."

" What do you mean, silly boy ? " she
    id, as an irregularity in the road threw
    er soft weight the more fondly upon my
    m.

" I mean, dear, that I want you to be my
ife."

" Your wife?   Not for worlds ! — no, forgive me, I did n't mean that.   You 're an
awful dear boy, and I like you very much,
and I think you 're rather fond of me ; but —

well, the truth is, I was never meant to be married, and don't care about it — and when you think of it, why should I?"

"You mean," I said, "that you are fortunate in living in a society where, as in heaven, there is neither marrying nor giving in marriage, where in fact nobody minds whether you're married or not, and where morals are very properly regarded as a personal and private matter —"

"Yes, that's what I mean," said Sylvia; "the people I care about — dear good people — will think no more of me for having a wedding-ring, and no less for my being without; and why should one put a yoke round one's neck when nobody expects it? A wedding-ring is like a top-hat, — you only wear it when you must — But it's very sweet of you, all the same, and you can kiss me if you like. Here's a nice sentimental patch of moonlight."

I really felt very dejected at this not of course entirely unexpected rejection, — if one might use the word for a situation on which had just been set the seal of so unmistakable a kiss; but the vision in my heart seemed to

smile at me in high and happy triumph. To
have won Sylvia would have been to have
lost her. My ideal had, as it were, held her
breath till Sylvia answered ; now she breathed
again.

" At all events, we can go on being chums,
can't we ? " I said.

For answer Sylvia hummed the first verse
of that famous song writ by Kit Marlowe.

" Yes ! " she said presently. " I will sing
for you, dance for you, and — perhaps — flirt
with you ; but marry you — no ! it 's best not,
for both of us."

" Well, then," I said, " dance for me ! You
owe me some amends for an aching heart."
As I said this, the path suddenly broadened
into a little circular glade into which the
moonlight poured in a silver flood. In the
centre of the space was a boulder some three
or four feet high, and with a flat slab-like
surface of some six feet or so.

" I declare I will," said Sylvia, giving me
an impulsive kiss, and springing on to the
stone ; " why, here is a ready-made stage."

" And there," I said, " are the nightingale
and the nightjar for orchestra."

"And there is the moon," said she, "for lime-light man."

"Yes," I said; "and here is a handful of glow-worms for the footlights."

, Then lifting up her heavy silk skirt about her, and revealing a paradise of chiffons, Sylvia swayed for a moment with her face full in the moon, and then slowly glided into the movements of a mystical dance.

It was thus the fountains were dancing to the moon in Arabia; it was thus the Nixies shook their white limbs on the haunted banks of the Rhine; it was thus the fairy women flashed their alabaster feet on the fairy hills of Connemara; it was thus the Houris were dancing for Mahomet on the palace floors of Paradise.

"It was over such dancing," I said, "that John the Baptist lost his head."

"Give me a kiss," she said, nestling exhausted in my arms. "I always want some one to kiss when I have danced with my soul as well as my body."

"I think we always do," I said, "when we've done anything that seems wonderful, that gives us the thrill of really doing —"

"And a poor excuse is better than none, is n't it, dear?" said Sylvia, her face full in the cataract of the moonlight.

As a conclusion for this chapter I will copy out a little song which I extemporised for Sylvia on our way home to Yellowsands — too artlessly happy, it will be observed, to rhyme correctly : —

> Sylvia 's dancing 'neath the moon,
>   Like a star in water;
> Sylvia 's dancing to a tune
>   Fairy folk have taught her.
>
> Glow-worms light her little feet
>   In her fairy theatre ;
> Oh, but Sylvia is sweet !
>   Tell me who is sweeter !

CHAPTER XII

AT THE CAFÉ DE LA PAIX

As love-making in which we have no share is apt to be either tantalising or monotonous, I propose to skip the next fortnight and introduce myself to the reader at a moment when I am once more alone. It is about six o'clock on a summer afternoon, I am in Paris, and seated at one of the little marble tables of the Café de la Paix, dreamily watching the glittering tide of gay folk passing by, —

> "All happy people on their way
> To make a golden end of day."

Meditatively I smoke a cigarette and sip a pale greenish liquor smelling strongly of aniseed, which is n't half so interesting as a commonplace whiskey and soda, but which, I am told, has the recommendation of being ten times as wicked. I sip it with a delicious thrill of degeneration, as though I were Eve tasting the apple for the first time, — for "such a power hath white simplicity." Sin is for the innocent, — a truth which sinners will be the first to regret. It was so, I said to myself, Alfred de Musset used to sit and sip his absinthe before a fascinated world. It is a privilege for the world to look on greatness at any moment, even when it is drinking. So I sat, and privileged the world.

It will readily be surmised from this exordium that — incredible as it may seem in a man of thirty — this was my first visit to Paris. You may remember that I had bought Orlando's tickets, and it had occurred to Sylvia aud me to use them. Sylvia was due in London to fulfil a dancing engagement within a fortnight after our arrival; so after a tender good-bye, which there was no earthly necessity to make final, I had remained behind for the purposes of study. Though, logically, my pilgrimage had ended with the unexpected discovery of Sylvia Joy, yet there were two famous feminine types of which, seeing that I was in Paris, I thought I might as well make brief studies, before I returned to London and finally resumed the bachelorhood from which I had started. These were the grisette of fiction and the American girl of fact. Pending these investigations, I meditated on the great city in the midst of which I sat.

A city! How much more it was than that! Was it not the most portentous symbol of modern history? Think what the word "Paris" means to the emancipated intellect, to the political government, to the humanised morals, of the world; not to speak of the romance of its literature, the tradition of its manners, and the immortal fame of its women. France is the brain of the world, as England is its heart, and Russia its fist. Strange is the power, strange are the freaks and revenges, of association, particularly perhaps of literary association. Here pompous official representatives may demur; but who can doubt that it is on its literature that a country must rely for its permanent representation? The countries that are forgotten, or are of no importance in the councils of the world, are countries without literature. Greece and Rome are more real in print than ever they were in marble. Though, as we know, prophets are not without honour save in their own countries and among their own kindred, the time comes when their countries and kindred are entirely without honour save by reason of those very prophets they once despised, rejected, stoned, and crucified. Subtract its great men from a nation, and where is its greatness?

Similarly, everything, however trifling, that has been written about, so long as it has been written about sufficiently well, becomes relatively enduring and representative of the country in which it is found. To an American, for example, the significance of a skylark is that Shelley sang it to skies where even it could never have mounted; and any one who has heard the nightingale must, if he be open-minded, confess its tremendous debt to Keats: a tenth part genuine song, the rest moon, stars, silence, and John Keats, — such is the nightingale. The real truth about a country will never be known till every representative type and condition in it have found their inspired literary mouthpiece. Meanwhile one country takes its opinion of another from the *aperçus* of a few brilliant but often irresponsible or prejudiced writers, — and really it is rather in what those writers leave out

than in what they put in that one must seek
the more reliable data of national character.

A quaint example of association occurs to
me from the experience of a friend of mine,
" rich enough to lend to the poor." Having
met an American friend newly landed at
Liverpool, and a hurried quarter of an hour
being all that was available for lunch, " Come
let us have a pork-pie and a bottle of Bass "
he had suggested.

"Pork-pies!" said the American, with a
delighted sense of discovering the country,—
"why, you read about them in Dickens!"
Who shall say but that this instinctive association was an involuntary severe, but not
inapplicable, criticism? A nightingale suggests Keats; a pork-pie, Dickens.

Similarly with absinthe, grisettes, the
Latin Quarter, and so on. Why, you read
about them in Murger, in Musset, in Balzac,
and in Flaubert; and the fact of your having
read about them is, I may add, their chief
importance.

So rambled my after-dinner reflections as
I sat that evening smoking and sipping,
sipping and smoking, at the Café de la Paix.

Presently in my dream I became aware of
English voices near me, one of which seemed
familiar, and which I could n't help over-
hearing. The voice of the husband said, —
you can never mistake the voice of the
husband, —

> 'T was the voice of the husband,
> I heard him complain, —

the voice of the husband said: "Dora, I for-
bid you! I will *not* allow my wife to be
seen again in the Latin Quarter. I permitted you to go once, as a concession, to
the Café d'Harcourt; but once is enough.
You will please respect my wishes!"

"But," pleaded the dear little woman,
whom I had an immediate impulse, Perseus-
like, to snatch from the jaws of her monster,
and turning to the other lady of the party of
four, — "but Mrs. —— has never been, and
she cannot well go without a chaperone.
Surely it cannot matter for once. It is n't
as if I were there constantly."

"No!" said the husband, with the absurd
pomposity of his tribe. "I 'm very sorry.
Mrs. —— will, of course, act as she pleases;
but I cannot allow you to do it, Dora."

At last the little wife showed some spirit.

"Don't talk to me like that, Will," she said. "I shall go if I please. Surely I am my own property."

"Not at all!" at once flashed out the husband, wounded in that most vital part of him, his sense of property. "There you mistake. You are *my* property, *my* chattel; you promised obedience to me; I bought you, and you do my bidding!"

"Great heavens!" I ejaculated, and, springing up, found myself face to face with a well-known painter whom you would have thought the most Bohemian fellow in London. And Bohemian he is; but Bohemians are seldom Bohemians for any one save themselves. They are terrible sticklers for convention and even etiquette in other people.

We recognised each other with a laugh, and presently were at it, hammer and tongs. I may say that we were all fairly intimate friends, and thus had the advantage of entire liberty of speech. I looked daggers at the husband; he looked daggers at me, and occasionally looking at his wife, gave her a

18

glance which was like the opening of Blue-
beard's closet. You could see the poor murdered bodies dangling within the shadowy
cupboard of his eye. Of course we got no
further. Additional opposition but further
enraged him. He recapitulated what he
would no doubt call his arguments, — they
sounded more like threats, — and as he spoke
I saw dragons fighting for their dams in the
primeval ooze, and heard savage trumpetings
of masculine monsters without a name.

I told him so.

"You are," I said, — "and you will forgive
my directness of expression, — you are the
Primeval Male! You are the direct descend-
ant of those Romans who carried off the
Sabine women. Nay! you have a much
longer genealogy. You come of those hairy
anthropoid males who hunted their mates
through the tangle of primeval forests, and
who finally obtained their consent — shall we
say? — by clubbing them on the head with a
stone axe. You talk a great deal of nonsense about the New Woman, but you,
Sir, are *The Old Male;* and," I continued,
"I have only to obtain your wife's con-

sent to take her under my protection this instant."

Curiously enough, "The Old Male," as he is now affectionately called, became from this moment quite a bosom friend.   Nothing would satisfy us but that we should all lodge at the same *pension* together, and there many a day we fought our battles over again. But that poor little wife never, to my knowledge, went to the Café d'Harcourt again.

CHAPTER XIII

THE INNOCENCE OF PARIS

THIS meeting with William and Dora was fortunate from the point of view of my studies; for that very night, as I dined with them *en pension*, I found that providence, with his usual foresight, had placed me next to a very charming American girl of the type that I was particularly wishful to study. She seemed equally wishful to be studied, and we got on amazingly from the first moment of our acquaintance. By the middle of dinner we were pressing each other's feet under the table, and when coffee and cigarettes had come, we were affianced lovers. "Why should I blush to own I love?" was evidently my quaint little companion's motto; and indeed she did n't blush to own it to the whole table, and publicly to announce that I was the dearest boy, and absolutely the most lovable man she had met.   There was nothing she would n't do for me.   Would she brave the terrors of the Latin Quarter with me, I asked, and introduce me to the terrible Café d'Harcourt, about which William and Dora had suffered such searchings of heart?   "Why, certainly; there was nothing in that," she said.   So we went.

Nothing is more absurd and unjust than those crude labels of national character which label one country virtuous and another vicious, one musical and another literary. Thus France has an unjust reputation for vice, and England an equally unjust reputation for virtue.

I had always, I confess, been brought up to think of Paris as a sort of Sodom and Gomorrah in one.   Good Americans might go to Paris, according to the American theory of a future state; but, certainly I had thought, no good Englishman ever went there—except, maybe, on behalf of the Vigilance Society.   Well, it may sound an odd thing to say, but what impressed me most of all was the absolute innocence of the place.

I mean this quite seriously. For surely one important condition of innocence is unconsciousness of doing wrong. The poor despised Parisian may be a very wicked and depraved person, but certainly he goes about with an absolute unconsciousness of it upon his gay and kindly countenance.

"Seeing the world" usually means seeing everything in it that most decent people won't look at; but when you come to look at these terrible things and places, what do you find? Why, absolute disappointment!

Have you ever read that most amusing book, "Baedeker on Paris"? I know nothing more delightful than the notes to the Montmartre and Latin Quarters. The places to which you, as a smug Briton, may or may not take a lady! The scale of wickedness allowed to the waxwork British lady is most charmingly graduated. I had read that the café where we were sitting was one of the most terrible places in Paris, — the Café d'Harcourt, where the students of the Latin Quarter take their nice little domestic mistresses to supper. But Baedeker was dreadfully Pecksniffian about these poor

innocent *étudiantes*, many of whom love
their lovers much more truly than many a
British wife loves her husband, and are
much better loved in return.   If you doubt
it, dare to pay attention to one of these
young ladies, and you will probably have to
fight a duel for it.   In fact, these romantic
relations are much more careful of honour
than conventional ones; for love, and not
merely law, keeps guard.

I looked around me.   Where were those
terrible things I had read of?   Where was
this hell which I had reasonably expected
would gape leagues of sulphur and blue
flame beneath the little marble table?   I
mentally resolved to bring an action against
Baedeker for false information.   For what
did I see?   Simply pairs and groups of
young men and women chattering amiably
in front of their "bocks" or their "Améri-
cains."   Here and there a student would
have his arm round a waist every one else
envied him.   One student was prettily trying a pair of new gloves upon his little
woman's hand.   Here and there blithe songs
would spring up, from sheer gladness of

heart; and never was such a buzz of happy
young people, not even at a Sunday-school
treat. To me it seemed absolutely Arcadian,
and I thought of Daphnis and Chloe and the
early world. Nothing indecorous or gross;
all perfectly pretty and seemly.

On our way home Semiramis was so sweet
to me, in her innocent, artless frankness,
that I went to bed with an intoxicating feeling that I must be irresistible indeed, to
have so completely conquered so true a
heart in so few hours. I was the more flattered because I am not a vain man, and am
not, like some, accustomed to take hearts as
the Israelites took Jericho with the blast of
one's own trumpet.

But, alas! my dream of universal irresisti-
bility was but short-lived, for next afternoon, as William and I sat out at some café
together, I found myself the object of chaff.

"Well," said William, "how goes the
love-affair?"

I flushed somewhat indignantly at his
manner with sanctities.

"I see!" he said, "I see! You are
already corded and labelled, and will be

shipped over by the next mail, — ' To Miss
Semiramis Wilcox, 1001 99th St., Philadel-
phia, U. S. A. *Man with care.*' Well, I
did think you'd got an eye in your head.
Look here, don't be a fool! I suppose she
said you were the first and last. The last
you certainly were. There are limits even
to the speed of American girls; but the
first, my boy! You are more like the twelfth,
to my ocular knowledge. Here comes
Dubois the poet. He can tell you something about Miss Semiramis. Eh! Dubois,
you know Miss Semiramis Wilcox, don't
you?"

The Frenchman smiled and shrugged.

"Un peu," he said.

"Don't be an ass and get angry," William
continued; "it's all for your own good."

"The little Semiramis has been seducing
my susceptible friend here. Like many of
us, he has been captivated by her naturalness,
her naïveté, her clear good eyes, — that look
of nature that is always art! May I relate
the idyl of your tragic passion, dear Dubois,
as an object lesson?"

The Frenchman bowed, and signed William
to proceed.

"You dined with us one evening, and you thus met for the first time. You sat together at table. What happened with the fish?"

"She swore I was the most beautiful man she had ever seen, — and I am not beautiful, as you perceive."

If not beautiful, the poet was certainly true.

"What happened at the entrée?"

"Oh, long before that we were pressing our feet under the table."

"And the coffee —"

"Mon Dieu! we were Tristram and Yseult, we were all the great lovers in the Pantheon of love."

"And what then?"

"Oh, we went to the Café d'Harcourt — mon ami."

"Did she wear a veil?" I asked.

"Oui, certainement!"

"And did you say, 'Why do you wear a veil, — setting a black cloud before the eyes and gates of heaven'?"

"The very words," said the Frenchman.

"And did she say, 'Yes, but the veil can be raised?'"

"She did, mon pauvre ami," said the poet.

"And did you raise it?"

"I did," said the poet.

"And so did I," I answered. And as I spoke, there was a crash of white marble in my soul, and lo! Love had fallen from his pedestal and been broken into a thousand pieces, — a heavy, dead thing he lay upon the threshold of my heart.

We had appointed a secret meeting in the salon of the *pension* that afternoon. I was not there! (Nor, as I afterwards learnt, was Semiramis.) When we did meet, I was brutally cold. I evaded all her moves; but when at last I decided to give her a hearing, I confess it needed all my cynicism to resist her air of innocence, of pathetic devotion.

If I couldn't love her, she said, might she go on loving me? Might she write to me sometimes? She would be content if now and again I would send her a little word. Perhaps in time I would grow to believe in her love, etc.

The heart-broken abandonment with which she said this was a sore trial to me; but

though love may be deceived, vanity is ever
vigilant, and vanity saved me.   Yet I left her
with an aching sense of having been a brute,
and on the morning of my departure from
Paris, as I said good-bye to William and
Dora, I spoke somewhat seriously of Semiramis.   Dora, Dora-like, had believed in her
all along, — not having enjoyed William's
opportunities of studying her, — and she
reproached me with being rather hard-
hearted.

"Nonsense," said William, "if she really
cared, would n't she have been up to bid you
good-bye?"

The words were hardly gone from his lips
when there came a little knock at the door.
It was Semiramis; she had come to say good-
bye.   Was it in nature not to be touched?
"Good-bye," she said, as we stood a moment
alone in the hall.   "I shall always think of
you; you shall not be to me as a ship that
has passed in the night, though to me you
have behaved very like an iceberg."

We parted in tears and kisses, and I lived
for some weeks with that sense of having been
a Nero, till two months after I received a

much glazed and silvered card to the usual effect.

And so I ceased to repine for the wound I had made in the heart of Semiramis Wilcox.

Of another whom I met and loved in that brief month in Paris, I cherish tenderer memories. Prim little Pauline Deschapelles! How clearly I can still see the respectable brass plate on the door of your little flat — " Mademoiselle Deschapelles — Modes et Robes ; " and indeed the " modes et robes " were true enough. For you were in truth a very hard-working little dressmaker, and I well remember how impressed I was to sit beside you, as you plied your needle on some gown that must be finished by the evening, and meditate on the quaint contrast between your almost Puritanic industry and your innocent love of pleasure. I don't think I ever met a more conscientious little woman than little Pauline Deschapelles.

There was but one drawback to our intercourse. She did n't know a word of English, and I could n't speak a word of French. So we had to make shift to love without either language. But sometimes Pauline would

throw down her stitching in amused impatience, and, going to her dainty secretaire,
write me a little message in the simplest
baby French — which I would answer in
French which would knit her brows for a
moment or two, and then send her off in
peals of laughter.

It *was* French! I know. Among the
bric-à-brac of my heart I still cherish some
of those little slips of paper with which
we made international love — question and
answer.

"Vous allez m'oublier, et ne plus penser à
moi — ni me voir. Les hommes — égoïstes —
menteurs, pas dire la vérité . . . " so ran the
questions, considerably devoid of auxiliary
verbs and such details of construction.

"Je serais jamais t'oublier," ran the frightful
answers!

Dear Pauline! Shall I ever see her again?
She was but twenty-six. She may still live.

CHAPTER XIV

END OF BOOK THREE

So ended my pilgrimage. I had wandered far, had loved many, but I came back to London without the Golden Girl. I had begun my pilgrimage with a vision, and it was with a vision that I ended it. From all my goings to and fro upon the earth, I had brought back only the image of a woman's face, — the face of that strange woman of the moorland, still haunting my dreams of the night and the day.

It was autumn in my old garden, damp and forsaken, and the mulberry-tree was hung with little yellow shields. My books looked weary of awaiting me, and they and the whole lonely house begged me to take them where sometimes they might be handled by human fingers, mellowed by lamplight, cheered by friendly laughter.

The very chairs begged mutely to be sat upon, the chill white beds to be slept in. Yes,

the very furniture seemed even lonelier than
myself.

So I took heed of their dumb appeal.

" I know," I answered them tenderly, — " I
too, with you, have looked on better days, I
too have been where bells have knoll'd to
church, I too have sat at many a good man's
feast, — yes! I miss human society, even as
you, my books, my bedsteads, and my side-
boards, — so let it be. It is plain our little
Margaret is not coming back, our little Margaret, dear haunted rooms, will never come
back; no longer shall her little silken figure
flit up and down your quiet staircases, her
hands filled with flowers, and her heart humming with little songs. Yes, let us go, it is very
lonely; we shall die if we stay here all so
lonely together; it is time, let us go."

So thereon I wrote to a furniture-remover,
and went out to walk round the mossy old
garden for the last time, and say good-bye to
the great mulberry, under whose Dodonaesque
shade we had sat half frightened on starry
nights, to the apple-trees whose blossom had
seemed like fairy-land to Margaret and me,
town-bred folk, to the apricots and the peaches

and the nectarines that it had seemed almost wicked to own, — as though we had gone abroad in silk and velvet, — to the little grassy orchard, and to the little green corner of it, where Margaret had fallen asleep that summer afternoon, in the great wicker-chair, and I had brought a dear friend on tiptoe to gaze on her asleep, with her olive cheeks delicately flushed, her great eyelids closed like the cheeks of roses, and her gold hair tumbled about her neck . . .

Well, well, good-bye, — tears are foolish things. They will not bring Margaret back. Good-bye, old garden, good-bye, I shall never see you again, — good-bye.

19

BOOK IV

THE POSTSCRIPT TO A PILGRIMAGE

CHAPTER I

SIX YEARS AFTER

THIS book is like a woman's letter. The most important part of it is the postscript.

Six years lie between the end of the last chapter and the beginning of this. Meanwhile, I had moved to sociable chambers within sound of the city clocks, and had lived the life of a lonely man about town, sinking more and more into the comfortable sloth of bachelorhood. I had long come to look back upon my pilgrimage as a sort of Indian-summer youth, being, as the reader can reckon for himself, just on thirty-seven. As one will, with one's most serious experiences, hastening

to laugh lest one should weep, as the old
philosopher said, I had made some fun out
of my quest, in the form of a paper for a
bookish society to which I belonged, on
"*Woman as a Learned Pursuit.*" It is
printed among the transactions of the society, and is accessible to the curious only by
loan from the members, and I regret that I
am unable to print any extracts here. Perhaps when I am dead the society will see the
criminal selfishness of reserving for itself what
was meant for mankind.

Meanwhile, however, it is fast locked and
buried deep in the archives of the club.
I have two marriages to record in the in-
terval: one that of a young lady whom I
must still think of as 'Nicolete' to Sir Mar-
maduke Pettigrew, Bart., of Dultowers Hall,
and the other the well-known marriage of
Sylvia Joy . . .

Sylvia Joy married after all her fine prot-
estations! Yes! but I 'm sure you will forgive her, for she was married to a lord.
When one is twenty and romantic one would
scorn a woman who would jilt us for wealth
and position; at thirty, one would scorn any

woman who did n't. Ah me! how one
changes! No one, I can honestly say, was
happier over these two weddings than I, and
I sent Sylvia her petticoat as a wedding
present.

* * * * *

But it was to tell of other matters that I
reopen this book and once more take up my
pen — matters so near to my heart that I
shrink from writing of them, and am half
afraid that the attempt may prove too hard
for me after all, and my book end on a
broken cry of pain. Yet, at the same time,
I want to write of them, for they are beautiful
and solemn, and good food for the heart.

Besides, though my pilgrimage had been
ended so long, they are really a part, yea,
the part for which, though I knew it not, all
the rest has been written — for they tell how
I came to find by accident her whom so long
I had sought of design.

How shall I tell of Thee who, first and last
of all women, gave and awoke in me that love
which is the golden key of the world, the
mystic revelation of the holy meaning of life,
love that alone may pass through the awful

gates of the stars, and gaze unafraid into the blue abysses beyond?

Ah! Love, it seemed far away indeed from the stars, the place where we met, and only by the light of love's eyes might we have found each other — as only by the light of love's eyes . . . But enough, my Heart, the world waits to hear our story, — the world once so unloving to you, the world with a heart so hard and anon so soft for love. When the story is ended, my love, when the story is ended —

CHAPTER II

GRACE O' GOD

IT was a hard winter's night four years ago, lovely and merciless ; and towards midnight I walked home from a theatre to my rooms in St. James's Street. The Venusberg of Piccadilly looked white as a nun with snow and moonlight, but the melancholy music of pleasure, and the sad daughters of joy, seemed not to heed the cold. For another hour death and pleasure would dance there beneath the electric lights.

Through the strange women clustering at the corners I took my way, — women of the Moabites, Ammonites, Edomites, Zidonians, and Hittites, — and I thought, as I looked into their poor painted faces, — faces but half human, vampirish faces, faces already waxen with the look of the grave, — I thought, as I often did, of the poor little girl whom De Quincey loved, the good-hearted little 'peri-

patetic' as he called her, who had succoured
him during those nights, when, as a young
man, he wandered homeless about these very
streets, — that good, kind little Ann whom De
Quincey had loved, then so strangely lost,
and for whose face he looked into women's
faces as long as he lived.   Often have I stood
at the corner of Titchfield Street, and thought
how De Quincey had stood there night after
night waiting for her to come, but all in vain,
and how from the abyss of oblivion into
which some cruel chance had swept her, not
one cry from her ever reached him again.

I thought, too, as I often did, what if the
face I seek should be here among these poor
outcasts, — golden face hidden behind a mask
of shame, true heart still beating true even
amidst this infernal world!

Thus musing, I had walked my way out of
the throng, and only a figure here and there
in the shadows of doorways waited and waited
in the cold.

It was something about one of these waiting figures, — some movement, some chance
posture, — that presently surprised my attention and awakened a sudden sense of half-

recognition. She stood well in the shadow, seeming rather to shrink from than to court attention. As I walked close by her and looked keenly into her face, she cast down her eyes and half turned away. Surely, I had seen that tall, noble figure somewhere before, that haughty head ; and then with the apparition a thought struck me — but, no! it could n't be she! not *here !*

" It is," said my soul, as I turned and walked past her again; " you missed her once, are you going to miss her again?"

" It is," said my eyes, as they swept her for the third time; " but she had glorious chestnut hair, and the hair of this woman is — gilded."

" It is she," said my heart; " thank God, it is she ! "

So it was that I went up to that tall, shy figure.

" It must be very cold here," I said; " will you not join me in some supper?"

She assented, and we sought one of the many radiating centres of festivity in the neighbourhood. She was very tired and cold,

— so tired she seemed hardly to have the spirit to eat, and evidently the cold had taken tight clutch of her lungs, for she had a cough that went to my heart to hear, and her face was ghastly pale. When I had persuaded her to drink a little wine, she grew more animated and spots of suspicious colour came into her cheeks. So far she had seemed all but oblivious of my presence, but now she gave me a sweet smile of gratitude, one of those irradiating transfiguring smiles that change the whole face, and belong to few faces, the heavenly smile of a pure soul.

Yes, it was she! The woman who sat in front of me was the woman whom I had met so strangely that day on that solitary moorland, and whom in prophecy still more strange my soul had declared to be, "now and for ever and before all worlds the woman God had created for me, and that unless I could be hers and she mine, there could be no home, no peace, for either of us so long as we lived —" and now so strangely met again.

Yes, it was she!

For the moment my mind had room for no other thought. I cared not to conjecture by

what devious ways God had brought her to
my side. I cared not what mire her feet had
trodden. She had carried her face pure as a
lily through all the foul and sooty air. There
was a pure heart in her voice. Sin is of the
soul, and this soul had not sinned! Let him
that is without sin amongst you cast the first
stone.

" Why did you dye that wonderful chestnut hair?" I asked her presently — and was
sorry next minute for the pain that shot across
her face, but I just wanted to hint at what I
designed not to reveal fully till later on, and
thus to hint too that it was not as one of the
number of her defilers that I had sought her.

" Why," she said, " how do you know the
colour of my hair? We have never met
before."

" Yes, we have," I said, " and that was why
I spoke to you to-night. I 'll tell you where
it was another time."

But after all I could not desist from telling
her that night, for, as afterwards at her lodg-
ing we sat over the fire, talking as if we had
known each other all our lives, there seemed
no reason for an arbitrary delay.

I described to her the solitary moorland road, and the grey-gowned woman's figure in front of me, and the gig coming along to meet her, and the salutation of the two girls, and I told her all one look of her face had meant for me, and how I had wildly sought her in vain, and from that day to this had held her image in my heart.

And as I told her, she sobbed with her head against my knee, and her great hair filling my lap with gold. In broken words she drew for me the other side of the picture of that long-past summer day.

Yes, the girl in the gig was her sister, and they were the only daughters of a farmer who had been rich once, but had come to ruin by drink and misfortune. They had been brought up from girls by an old grandmother, with whom the sister was living at the time of my seeing them. Yes, Tom was her husband. He was a doctor in the neighbourhood when he married her, and a man, I surmised, of some parts and promise, but, moving to town, he had fallen into loose ways, taken to drinking and gambling, and had finally deserted her for another woman — at the very moment

when their first child was born. The child
died —

" Thank God ! " she added with sudden
vehemence, and " I — well, you will wonder how I came to this, I wonder myself —
it has all happened but six months ago, and yet
I seem to have forgotten — only the broken-
hearted and the hungry would understand, if
I could remember — and yet it was not life,
certainly not life I wanted — and yet I could n't
die — "

The more I came to know Elizabeth and
realise the rare delicacy of her nature, the
simplicity of her mind, and the purity of her
soul, the less was I able to comprehend the
psychology of that false step which her great
misery had forced her to take. For hers was
not a sensual, pleasure-loving nature. In fact,
there was a certain curious Puritanism about
her, a Puritanism which found a startlingly
incongruous and almost laughable expression
in the Scripture almanac which hung on the
wall at the end of her bed, and the Bible, and
two or three Sunday-school stories which,
with a copy of " Jane Eyre," were the only
books that lay upon the circular mahogany
table.

Once I ventured gently to chaff her about this religiosity of hers.

"But surely you believe in God, dear," she had answered, "you're not an atheist!"

I think an atheist, with all her experience of human monsters, was for her the depth of human depravity.

"No, dear," I had answered; "if *you* can believe in God, surely I can!"

I repeat that this gap in Elizabeth's psychology puzzled me, and it puzzles me still, but it puzzled me only as the method of working out some problem which after all had "come out right" might puzzle one. It was only the process that was obscure. The result was gold, whatever the dark process might be. Was it simply that Elizabeth was one of that rare few who can touch pitch and not be defiled? — or was it, I have sometimes wondered, an unconscious and after all a sound casuistry that had saved Elizabeth's soul, an instinctive philosophy that taught her, so to say, to lay a Sigurd's sword between her soul and body, and to argue that nothing can defile the body without the consent of the soul.

In deep natures there is always what one might call a lover's leap to be taken by those that would love them — something one cannot understand to be taken on trust, something even that one fears to be gladly adventured . . . all this, and more, I knew that I could safely venture for Elizabeth's sake, ere I kissed her white brow and stole away in the early hours of that winter's morning.

As I did so I had taken one of the sumptuous strands of her hair into my hand and kissed it too.

" Promise me to let this come back to its own beautiful colour," I had said, as I nodded to a little phial labelled " Peroxide of Hydrogen " on her mantelshelf.

" Would you like to ? " she had said.

" Yes, do it for me."

One day some months after I cut from her dear head one long thick lock, one half of which was gold and the other half chestnut. I take it out and look at it as I write, and, as when I first cut it, it seems still a symbol of Elizabeth's life, the sun and the shadow, only that the gold was the shadow, and the chestnut was the sun.

The time came when the locks, from crown to tip, were all chestnut — but when it came I would have given the world for them to be gold again; for Elizabeth had said a curious thing when she had given me her promise.

"All right, dear," she had said, " but something tells me that when they are all brown again our happiness will be at an end."

" How long will that take?" I had said, trying to be gay, though an involuntary shudder had gone through me, less at her words than because of the strange conviction of her manner.

"About two years, — perhaps a little more," she said, answering me quite seriously, as she gravely measured the shining tresses, half her body's length, with her eye.

CHAPTER III

THE GOLDEN GIRL

ONE fresh and sunny morning, some months after this night, Elizabeth and I stood before the simple altar of a little country church, for the news had come to us that her husband was dead, and thus we were free to belong to each other before all the world. The exquisite stillness in the cool old church was as the peace in our hearts, and the rippling sound of the sunlit leaves outside seemed like the very murmur of the stream of life down which we dreamed of gliding together from that hour.

It was one of those moments which sometimes come and go without any apparent cause, when life suddenly takes a mystical aspect of completeness, all its discords are harmonised by some unseen hand of the spirit, and all its imperfections fall away. The lover of beauty and the lover of God alike know these strange moments, but none know them with such a mighty satisfaction as a man and a woman who love as loved Elizabeth and I.

Love for ever completes the world, for it is no future of higher achievement, no expectation of greater joy. It lives for ever in a present made perfect by itself. Love can dream of no greater blessedness than itself, of no heaven but its own. God himself could have added no touch of happiness to our happy hearts that grave and sunny morning. You philosophers who go searching for the meaning of life, thinkers reading so sadly, and let us hope so wrongly, the riddle of the world — life has but one meaning, the riddle but one answer — which is Love. To love is to put yourself in harmony with the spheral music of creation, to stand in the centre of the universe, and see it good and whole as it appears in the eye of God.

Even Death himself, the great and terrible King of kings, though he may break the heart of love with agonies and anguish and slow tortures of separation, may break not his faith. No one that has loved will dream

even death too terrible a price to pay for the
revelation of love. For that revelation once
made can never be recalled. As a little sprig
of lavender will perfume a queen's wardrobe,
so will a short year of love keep sweet a long
life. And love's best gifts death can never
take away. Nay, indeed, death does not so
much rob as enrich the gifts of love. The
dead face that was fair grows fairer each
spring, sweet memories grow more sweet,
what was silver is now gold, and as years
go by, the very death of love becomes its
immortality.

I think I shall never hear Elizabeth's voice
again, never look into her eyes, never kiss
her dear lips — but Elizabeth is still mine,
and I am hers, as in that morning when we
kissed in that little chancel amid the flicker-
ing light, and passed out into the sun and
down the lanes, to our little home among the
meadow-sweet.

She is still as real to me as the stars, —
and, alas, as far away! I think no thought
that does not fly to her, I have no joys I do
not share with her, I tell her when the spring
is here, and we sit beneath the moon and

listen to the nightjar together. Sometimes we are merry together as in the old time, and our laughter makes nightfaring folk to cross themselves; my work, my dreams, my loves, are all hers, and my very sins are sinned for her sake.

Two years did Elizabeth and I know the love that passeth all understanding, and day by day the chestnut upon her head was more and the gold less, till the day came that she had prophesied, and with the day a little child, whose hair had stolen all her mother's gold, as her heart had drained away her mother's life.

Ah! reader, may it be long before you kneel at the bedside of her you love best in the world, and know that of all your love is left but a hundred heart-beats, while opposite sits Death, watch in hand, and fingers upon her wrist.

" Husband," whispered Elizabeth, as we looked at each other for the last time, " let her be your little golden girl . . . "

And then a strange sweetness stole over her face, and the dream of Elizabeth's life was ended.

As I write I hear in the still house the running of little feet, a fairy patter sweet and terrible to the heart.

Little feet, little feet — perhaps if I follow you I shall find again our mother that is lost. Perhaps Elizabeth left you with me that I should not miss the way.

www.ingramcontent.com/pod-product-compliance
Lightning Source LLC
Chambersburg PA
CBHW060542030726
47498CB00004B/1284